LOVERS AND HERETICS

LOVERS AND HERETICS

by
JOHN HALE

The Dial Press / James Wade
New York
1978

c.1

Published by
The Dial Press/James Wade
1 Dag Hammarskjold Plaza
New York, New York 10017

Originally published in Great Britain by Victor Gollancz Ltd., London.

Manufactured in the United States of America

First U.S.A. printing

Library of Congress Cataloging in Publication Data

Hale, John.
Lovers and heretics.

Reprint of the ed. published by V. Gollancz, London.
I. Title.
PZ4.H163Lq 1978   [PR6058.A438]   823'.9'14   77-27096
ISBN 0-8037-4771-3

/3L

AUG 28 '78

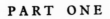

PART ONE

Political/moral themes underlie this story of a British soldier and a Holocaust survivor and their friendship.

BERLIN. IN THE early sixties.

Christmas. Heiliger Abend and twenty below. Thick and beautiful the snow in the streets. Strong legs needed and boots over the ankles to march through it across muffled crossings down long streets through air like lead to find cinemas, eating places underground steaming warm to pack the belly.

A concert. Hey! Jacko! Come and work the tape recorder, pull the curtain, get a close-up of officers' crumpet. I don't mind if I do. Gives you a cheap thrill, Jacko, and that poof at the piano's bloody funny you ever heard anything like it, mate? I think he fancies you, Jacko, the way he yells up at you. Piss off before I thump you. You and who's army? Not the Yanks, I tell you that!

He was something to do with the British Council. It was never made clear. With Frank and his friends of those days nothing was ever quite clear. It went with the atmosphere of the city at that time. The Wall was up sealing off the East. It was sometimes possible to escape then. The killing technique was not perfected.

In the west zone it was like being on drugs all the time. Edgy and overstimulated. You got the impression that the lights in the Ku-damm burned brighter, strobed at a higher frequency than any other—a sort of continuous dazzle. To be 22 years old, fit, bursting to put it somewhere not just the urgent pecker but all the rest, maelstrom of feelings and unexpressed, unexpressable desires swirling like the snow out of the darkness.

Jack measures his life in triggers to action. They come years apart, unlooked for, recognized with hindsight as inevitable. Only one had taken place so far. Jack joined the army, fled the village into the wider world. Frank was the second. Frank was the poof at the piano.

*   *   *

7

Rather than be on his own for five minutes Frank would cross a minefield for company. Any company. The intensity of this need was greater in him than self preservation.

Frank's friends were mysterious to Jack not because of their characters but because of Jack's ignorance. Jack did not read, knew no history. But he was ambitious; he had the makings of a fine social and intellectual snob. Jack also was secretive. It flattered something in him to sit silent in the darkest corner and listen and observe. Jack was waiting for something.

Even before he was posted to Berlin he began to write things down. His feelings, his ideas. He told himself the story of his life in his head. At first it was a very short story—but it grew! Jack did not like to tell himself the parts of his life when he was not a hero. When he masturbated a whole year almost every day and could not stop and his cock got a bend in it from his urgent grip.

Frank's friends were mysterious but not threatening to Jack. He was already past the stage where he wanted to destroy, or ignore, what he did not understand. He wanted to understand.

The mystery drew him to it. It fascinated him like the mystery of love, the mystery of art, the mystery of religion. It was none of these. It was politics. European and emigré.

Jack understands these things imperfectly even now. Although they have germinated in the deeps of his mind for fifteen years. The news of Frank's death brings them, fragmented, to the surface. He must piece them together.

When I try to put down what happened, what was said and done in Berlin, in a derelict town on the Kentish coast and other places remembered not by name but by violent events I am conscious of continual distortion.

I say aloud, "It was not like that, why am I pretending it was?"

Then I understand that in me is this censor, this liar, this coward.

To overcome it I must often speak of myself in the third person. I write: Jack is not sure why he made the journey ... and in this way I am sufficiently freed from Jack to report him

8

without too much feeling; without being too ashamed when he is much less than a hero.

At an earlier, less menacing time, I think I would have accepted Frank's death as the accident it was reported to be. I would not have made the journey. Had I, by some other chance, met the woman I would have noticed her but passed her by. It turned out that I had done that once but forgotten.

But a sense of the coming wrath which touched us all at this time both sharpened and distorted the senses.

Berlin.

After the Christmas concert, the party. Everyone in plain clothes but knowing the ranks exactly. An erotic undertow. I had a girl in England at that time. Long-legged Jenny who wore funny hats to keep up her morale on the bad days. A country girl from Wiltshire not really happy in the town. Sometimes she cried for no reason. Most of the time she was so full of life and sympathy that old ladies, drunks, stray dogs and neurotic children homed on her from streets away. I don't know where that put me.

I seemed set upon a certain kind of woman from the village days on. She was not at this party this Jack-type woman. So he left. Half cut and out into the snow. Left, right, left, right.

After a mile the car slid up beside me scattering snow. Frank wound down the window and stuck his head out. He wore a fur hat. He would.

"Give you a lift, Jack?"

"No."

"Why not?"

"I like the weather, sir."

"Don't be a cunt calling me 'sir', Jack—call me Frank."

"I like the weather, Frank."

"Come on, hop in. I can't stick my own company."

He was grinning at me. Jack thought if the worst comes to the worst and he tries to tap me up I'll have to thump him. But he's a cheerful bugger and it's Christmas so here we go, Glad, and don't let your mates know or they'll tab me for a nancy boy.

He drove with no idea how a car works. Say what you like

9

about British engineering that particular gearbox deserved a Queen's award. It was an old Ford Popular, I mean old even then and it rocked like hell on the corners. He bought it off his cousin he told me as if that meant something. He giggled like a schoolgirl in the skids and slides.

"You'll get pinched."

"I should be so lucky."

"Did you drive this from England?"

In the rehearsals for the concert we'd been given his Noël Coward voice and his Max Miller and his George Formby while he sat sorting out the music. He wrote the music cribbed from lots of other people's music spread all round the upright. He did instant composition (prepared the night before) "What we want here, kiddoes, is a little pastiche Cole Porter something like this."

He also had an all-purpose American voice. It was terrible. He was very proud of it. It was based on Andy Devine and if you never saw Andy Devine you missed a treat.

"Sure as hell diyud," he said, "I druv this lil ol beauty clear cross from Lunnon, England, Jack ma boy."

"Oh yes."

"Yes—have you a secret sorrow?"

"What?"

"You had the attitude, this evening, of a costive rhino. At the party you were enveloped in a dark haze—is there trouble back at t'mill, lad?"

"I miss my girl."

"Ah!"

"I wouldn't mind getting home to Mum and Dad for Christmas, either."

"Ah!"

"And I'm sorry I joined; dear Mum, sell the pig and buy me out."

"Why did you join?"

You don't tell a stranger a story like that. Besides he did not want to hear.

"Why," Frank said to himself, "does anybody join the army voluntarily? I was in during the war, of course. A friendly alien. The pioneer corps. I was a coward from my youth up and they sensed that. They sent me to safe places, while all around me others volunteered to de-fuse bombs and leap back into Germany on the end of parachutes. Of course being an Austrian Jew with a certain name——" he paused dramatically. Quite often his sense of drama swamped his sense of humour. There was nothing Jack could say.

"The name was on the list, you see," he went on as if I would immediately understand. I nodded and looked interested.

"The *Sonderfahndungsliste GB*, you know? A list of persons to be immediately arrested and handed over to the Gestapo when the Germans invaded. I was well down. To be handed over to Department IV of the Central Reich Security Office. Fairly well down, but *there*—an honour in a way but due entirely to my mother. Of course they were very inefficient, the Nazis you know that?—it was my mother's *own name*, maiden name, not mine at all. She was always emancipated. So I'm told. She actually married my father only after terrible pressure from her own family; the Jewish side, you see? But always used her own name *politically*."

"So it wasn't your name on the list," said Jack having understood that much.

"No," replied Frank, "and the list itself was not known to us until after the war, in 1945."

"So," said Jack, "none of that could have had much to do with where you were posted."

"You are right," said Frank generously, "and had I been captured I might well have got away with it under the Geneva Convention don't you think?"

This conclusion made him thoughtful. It also made him take a left turn on the wrong side of the road and nearly get us killed. I shouted at him as he scraped past the inevitable Mercedes taxi. It was going hard on the horn which made a magnificent doppler effect as we slid by. It put its lights full up at the same time just to make sure by blinding us that any crash would be fatal. We got away with it.

"The trouble is," said Frank, "I sometimes get carried away with my past."

Before I could reply he said, "You need a drink, Jack—we both need a drink. I wouldn't be surprised if that taxi driver was ex Waffen SS, a good thing my reflexes are what they are."

"You were on the wrong side of the road you silly sod," I said because my knees were still shaking and my heart was choking me.

He took both hands off the wheel clapped them and shouted with laughter.

"I never knew you cared, dearie," he said, "play it again, Sam."

I punched his arm and said, "Get hold of the bloody wheel, Frank, will you, I'm too young to die."

"And far too pretty," he said. "I'll drive if you'll stop hitting me and using foul language—it's dreadfully upsetting to an artiste of my sensibilities you military prick, you!"

The snow was falling again as if someone had twirled the glass globe and set it down. The buildings where we stopped were of a dirty-brown stone. The snow and the light from the lamps made them look like dried blood. There were iron grilles on the ground-floor windows and some of the walls were still bullet marked and chipped from shell bursts. When we got out of the car everything was muffled by the snow and when you looked up it fell softly on your face from the enormous outer darkness beyond the upward glow of the city.

Frank said, "I never pass this," he indicated the damaged walls, "without thinking of the Gestapo, they had a place here, on this corner. I have a friend who is psychic. When he came to see me I never told him about it. But when he passed the place he stopped and became ill instantly rather the way people have a heart attack. The vile things that happened to people in there have remained in the stone. He picked up the wave lengths. It attacked him. Did you know that even voices do that? Imprint themselves in surrounding material shifting the molecules?"

I looked to see if he was serious. He seemed to be.

"I'd like to invent a machine to decode the Parthenon," he said.

Frank spoke in long monologues as a method of making decisions or forming and clarifying ideas. He made it appear that he was conducting a conversation. It was nearly always a personal enquiry.

His relationship with Jack at that time depended on Jack's natural inclination to be a good listener.

Frank was the guide for whom Jack did not know he was looking.

Jack comforted Frank because he made no judgements. Jack knew instinctively those areas he must never bear upon because Frank was capable of uncontrollable, sometimes murderous frenzies if some nerve to his appalling childhood was touched. Jack had the same knack with his mother over the drinking and the money worries.

Jack was overwhelmed by Frank's world when he first entered it.

He lived in a flat off a concrete landing three flights up with a spyhole in the door.

"I borrowed this place, he's away three months come in, come in, let me get you a drink I know I need one."

"After that taxi."

"After that party!"

He avoided the music that was scattered everywhere—sheet music, scores bound in leather, records in their sleeves, records out of their sleeves which lay, like a random gallery of pop art across the surfaces of chairs, tables, piano top, even balanced on the rows of books packed on shelves. Lamps on low tables, lamps on the floor, light catching the edge of enormous orange cushions. It seemed to Jack a cross between a fantasy and a knocking shop. The colours made his mouth water like sweets in the village shop. Chocolate walls, greens from the throats of ducks shimmering, book jackets, lamp shades and, where there was space, long reproduction posters of sexy bints, French and flowing; luscious armfuls from naughty ninety days.

To the village puritan such a sense of inviting richness, almost decadence. A few years later half the kids' bedrooms in suburbia, UK carried the posters. But progress now is by geometric not arithmetic progression. How long since anyone, except the neglected old, were cold all day in winter and never expected it to be different? So it was when Jack was young a million years ago in 1947.

And overall the bloom of central heating and Frank offering

bottles as if he wanted to sell them to me. Picking them up, putting them down, reciting the names of whiskies and gins and vodkas and others I had never seen or heard of.

"He has a little drinking problem, my friend. He's gone to take the cure. It is disgusting. Aversion therapy. Drink and sick it up. Some of this? So will I. His hand shakes like an aspen until five minutes to noon. He kept off it in the mornings, you see, he even managed breakfast which was heroic—and then at twelve of the clock down goes the first double and within minutes he's as steady as a grenadier, whatever they may be—you are not one by any chance? No. Splendid! Try this, dear fellow, and do sit, the night is young, my God that party! What boring farts the British abroad no wonder Uncle Willie Maugham took his clever friend with him jaunting round the world to cheer him up; and how he managed to make all those sticks *interesting*! Now that is genius.

"You would think some of them would learn German, wouldn't you? I mean they patronize the Yanks—you notice I've caught it, *the Yanks*—for carting their refrigerated plastic hot dogs and portable air conditioning into the jungle, and having hypodermics plunged into their buuns at the first *sniff* of the common cold and there *they* are like something out of *Journey's End*—did you ever see it? It used to make Jonathan, my adopted Pa, rock with laughter in his day. Noël first found Johnnie Mills playing it in some far flung outpost—it is a play, by the way, I should have said that, a piece for the thee-ayter, my boy, in which the British are rather heroic and stiff upper except Stanhope who has hysterics. It was rather a fashion for the heroes of fiction in the twenties and thirties to have hysterics.

"Do sit down, and ignore it if the dust rises a little, oh you don't take soda; there's some ice somewhere for visiting Americans; no wonder they have needles plunged into them regularly like *assegais*—air conditioning positively shrivels the sinuses and the reason that dust clearly *is* rising all around is that I have, for days, locked out the cleaning *frau*.

"She drives me mad when I'm trying to work with my stuff spread about and she *clears*. I have to lock myself in the lavatory while outside the door, like the tartar horde, she levels everything before her. She leaves no book standing upon another. She sows the carpet with foaming cleaner—and she talks incessantly explaining quite often and in many different forms that neither she, nor anyone related to her, or known to her, or known to all of them ever harmed a hair on the head of a single Jew. Thus she destroys my concentration, an unfortunate word in this context, and ruins the comfort of my messy ways: the significant, private and symbolic, apparently random, patterns of sharpened pencils, books of reference, typewriter, notebooks, dictionary, cigarettes, matches, carbon paper, old toothbrushes for cleaning typefaces and a number of bottles of pills, a large bottle of mineral water, and——let me top you up, this is turning out rather well, don't you think? Far better than predatory army wives a-prowl and——I hope you are not married, Jack, if you are I withdraw just in time as the arch-deacon said to the counter tenor behind the mighty organ."

"No I'm not."

"Good, they are really obsessive."

"Army wives?"

"Germans like my cleaning *frau*. They simply cannot bear disorder and waste—that's why they turned us into soap and cooking fats and the occasional, one off, lampshade. Disorder and waste ruins their digestions and they can't enjoy all that delicious sausage and beer. I feel very guilty, dear motherly creature that she is, I don't wish to cause her sharp stabbing pains under the ribs after meals but in self defence, even if my dirty shirts are piling up——but that will do, move if you want to, clear a space, put your feet up, is it too hot? I can't stand central heating as a general rule but this isn't too aggressive—— did I mention that I am a writer?"

"Er—I don't think so, Frank."

"Ah. Material is everything, everything—I *understand* that but I don't *feel* it properly. What is lacking in me is the mental welder, no blinding blue flame of thought or intuition to weld together this man's twitch and that fellow's compulsive repetition of phrase; and size."

He leapt up and repeated, "Size," spreading his arms to indicate something vast and spilled his whisky over one of the cushions making dark patches on the orange. He paid no attention to that.

15

"A great book demands a great subject—you realise that of course?"

It would have been clear to someone of the most modest intelligence that the army corporal who sat gaping at Frank in Berlin that night was not, like the late disputed T. E. Lawrence, slumming in the ranks. If Jack, that confused non-com., had ever read a great book (other than *Treasure Island* which he got for Christmas when he was twelve) it would have been by mistake.

But Frank was not mocking Jack.

It was my good fortune that when conducting a monologue Frank was unable to imagine anyone within hearing who read, thought, observed less than himself. It was not a conscious, or self-conscious, lack of patronage—it was his way. It followed that Jack's silence must be an intelligent and appreciative silence. In fact Jack was interpreted as still water that runs . . . those beguiling depths into which many an ardent lover has dived only to crack his skull on the bottom of the empty pool. I ought to know. The miasma of sex and the sound of silence have had me running full pelt and naked along the top board for the plunge into the void—"Do you take this woman . . .?"

"Food," said Frank leaving the room talking, "and then the story of your life in every sordid detail. You are clearly a man of quality, not the eighteenth-century kind I grant you but out of the common run of licentious soldiery; I shall, in the brutal modern idiom, chat you up and pick your brains—there's delicacy for you, boy! Pick them over and make aspects of you immortal in my next *opus*."

His face came back round the door.

"Which I now confess, as you are clearly simpatico and would not betray a chum, is my *first opus*. Come out here to the kitchen I feel much better, now."

"Better?"

"The grapes of wrath!"

"What?"

"Piles, frightfully irritating, old horse, but never, never, never, Jack have the operation—not even if they are hanging down like bunches of grapes. I had a chum who had the operation and oh my God!"

"*Opus?*" I said helpfully because I did not want to hear what the operation did to his chum.

"*Opus. Opus* you are right, Jack, one must not be diverted. All effort to the *opus*. Every day the blank page in the typewriter but before the first thought forms itself Frau Attila the Hun has driven me with talk and Hoover into the last bunker. I wonder how much time Hitler spent on the lavatory in those final days? I brood over my mail in there. Please disregard it when you use the place, won't you?—it's there for comfort not for use although we do sometimes run out of the.... I find it soothing to be safe in the small room with letters and envelopes overlapping the trousers rumpled round the ankles—pages and pages in the familiar writing of friends and relatives."

"Every morning?"

"Yes!"

"But you have shut the *frau* out."

"That is true, but I find myself taking refuge all the same, you are on to it, Jack—clearly I am blocked! I must wait for the Id to speak."

In the narrow kitchen every surface was covered with dirty crockery. Plates and saucers projected dangerously over every edge. Odd knives and spoons lay on the floor among the English, German and American newspapers. The doors of wall cupboards stood ajar showing almost empty packets crumpled like concertinas. In the fridge was a litter of cartons and a solitary slice of bacon.

He strode in without flinching and from a corner picked up a tall bag of groceries.

"Food," he said, "bought this morning, more whisky while we work? We may even break into a brisk chorus of 'Jingle Bells' to celebrate the season, or possibly 'My Yiddisher Momma' —it comes but once a year they do say. Do you know that my Yiddisher Poppa is sufficiently assimilated to have the *tree* at Christmas if you take the point? He's a good man, Jonathan, one of those upper-middle-class English Jews, I mean two generations *at least* past the thought of his *kinder* having the operation—no, no, we all have that one, Jack—I refer to the nose job that uneasy yiddisher mommas save up for, not for themselves, dear heart, but for their daughters. To reduce the schonk

17

to acceptable Anglo-Saxon proportions——now where the hell is the cooking oil?"

He was suddenly angry. In that moment. Jack could not understand the change. Jack went past him into the kitchen and cleared and washed up. It took him twenty minutes. All that time Frank wandered in and out. Every now and again he spoke a name, or a phrase with a name in it. Jack did not catch the names. Later he met the people who owned them.

Jack sensed Frank's anger was to do with persecution; it was obvious enough but Jack was very ignorant of everything outside Jack's world. But his instinct was sound so as he washed up he told Frank about the first thing that happened to him after he joined up as a boy soldier when he was fifteen. He got beaten up for being filthy by the other lads. They scrubbed him with a yard broom in cold water with yellow soap. The reason Jack was filthy was they never had a bath in the cottage. Not a fixed bath. They had a tin bath brought in from the shed once a week. Jack's friendly mates scrubbed him raw. Jack kept both hands over his cock bent his head and cried all the time; there was so much noise and water they missed that. Afterwards Jack scrubbed himself every day under the shower. When he went on leave he noticed all the smells in the cottage for the first time in his life. It stank. This upset him more than the scrubbing. He said bad things to his parents in his shame.

Jack bided his time. After about a year he was in the back of an army truck going to a recruiting display by the parachute regiment on the downs at Bristol. The leader of the lads who scrubbed him leaned over the tailboard. Jack fell against him on a bend. He went over. He was in hospital three months and when he came out he never looked at Jack or said anything.

I laid the table.

Then we had eggs and bacon and black bread and pale butter and coffee and cream and whisky and export marmalade from a stone jar spread on export oat cakes. He was a terrible eater. He mopped up with bread, smoked all the time, tapped ash on the plate the minute he had finished, speckling the dry egg smears. He never said a word. I understood that. It has to work through you. Silence is best. Even if you are to be shot silence is best. You can hold yourself together.

Finished. Bloated. Sleepy.

He got up. Came round to me took hold of my hair in a handful and tugged so it lifted my skull.

"You can come again," he said, "as long as you do the washing up, kid." That was his Bogart voice.

Jack slept on the couch, untouched.

The derelict town on the Kentish coast.

It had some life about it once, this place where Frank died. It rose and fell with the empire.

For 300 years it had soldiers and sailors in the streets. It had bands and banners; the sounds of orders and gunfire and riots; the air was coloured with flags and pennants and the sun reflected by the killing steel of pikes, swords—and bayonets wavering in the heat haze, thick as a field of wheat above the marching heads of Englishmen.

There were whores and doss houses; folk crammed together upon hulks whose keels were gripped, until they rotted to skeletons, in the grey mud ooze that festered between the wash of tides.

On the town's edge the matted grass, half swamp, bred the mosquitoes for malaria and young and old they died, all part of the day's work; the survivors grew sturdy, or bent, to cheer the band join the colours salute the flag bend a stiff neck to God the Father, God of battles, and end up—some of them—carved on marble memorials in the garrison church.

In the music hall beyond the Wesleyan chapel, packed on Saturday nights with redcoats and bluejackets, full of smoke and stink the big woman, naked but for lace-up boots and a headdress, stood plump upon a pedestal while the band played and the gallant lads threw bottles at her. They fought in the alleys outside. They came to grips with the women, reeking and randy. They got crabs, clap and pox in that order. They went off to foreign parts and died for England, Home and Beauty without too much complaint. At least there is no record of it. Perhaps that is why Frank came here? To record, to celebrate even, this microcosm of the glory that has departed. It would have appealed to both his sense of irony and futility.

And the place now? A ghost of a town half derelict upon a promontory: a place now permanently impermanent—his own state made tangible: a place condemned, but in the still gentle political climate of this time its few survivors permitted their defiance. That would have appealed to him.

I can see that he might have found something here to make him rent one of the last weatherboard houses. Perhaps, at last, he began the book.

I stand on the site. I stir the recently water-logged, charred pieces and from them rises a sour and bitter smell. It is vile. Not exactly the aftermath of a Viking's funeral.

It is the morning of my first day in the place. Early. I drove in last night. It seems pointless now I am here. In fact it has every point. Yesterday I was in London. Yesterday I confronted Beatrice—Frank's sister, not by blood but by adoption. A terrible meeting. Today, without any doubt, Jonathan her father and Frank's adopted father will get in touch with me. I repeat the relationships because each time I have to convince myself of their reality.

But still against reason it feels pointless. I will do nothing irreversible, like contacting the police or the local paper, until Jonathan appears. I have to hear it from him. So—what to do?

I am uneasy standing in the open the only figure in a mouldering landscape. Yesterday was my first day of leave. They call it rest and recuperation leave. It comes about halfway through the tour in Ulster—and this is my second tour. By reflex I have noted where the sniper may lie. I am uneasy to be out in the open even in this place. A target.

It was not until an incident on my second tour in Belfast that I understood what Frank, his mother, his Jewish friends and relations endured in the Third Reich.

We patrolled. Search and lift. Sometimes we got killed. In the city and the rest of Ulster the Protestant Prods and the Catholic Provos went about their business according to their lights and the result was often hosed away it being too fragmented either to repair or go in a coffin. That is to be expected. What I refer to is an incident without casualties one afternoon.

We went single file near a Catholic school at going-home time. It was coming to dusk. The mothers and the aunts were waiting and the kids flooding out spreading across the road shouting. They had already had five years of the Troubles, these kids. They ran near the patrol; they jumped and bumped trying to tip off the berets, grab the rifles. Just a game, you might think. Then they ran clear, my lads having stopped, and their older mates who had the bricks in their hands and were in position flung them.

One of my lads got half a house-brick in the face and went down bleeding dropping his rifle. The nearest kid was not quick enough to get it. We got round to help, to guard his back, to look up at roof tops and windows for the barrel of a gun. It was the usual milling circus with the women screeching and the kids jeering.

You had to get it through your head that the women and the kids wanted you dead just as much as their husbands and fathers wanted you dead. It was hard to believe until you had the first real taste of it. The kids had managed it by themselves with an army driver a few weeks before. They smashed his windscreen with bricks, made him swerve—he died at the wheel. They killed him a treat and their mums gave them extra jam for tea.

I caught the one that threw the half house-brick. He was a stupid, thick set, little sod and ran the wrong way. He would not tell me his name and address but one of his treacherous mates obliged holding his mother's hand—and the mother looking at our lad with blood coming through his fingers and saying "Ah the poor feller, ah the poor feller" when you knew from what had happened with women like this before when they got their hands on a squaddie that she would have castrated him given a chance. If they fail to kill you they will lick your —— but there is too much feeling in this and the point to be made is quite a different one.

The simple fact is I walked him by the scruff of his shirt and jumper to his front door two streets away. I knocked and his mother came. She would not look at me. I told her I would not have kids doing to my lads what he had done. So who would beat him for it—her or me?

She took him in and beat him for getting caught.

What saved my neck, I suppose, was that the men were still at work, those who had a job; and there was not time to get word to the Tommy gun squad because what I had done was unexpected.

The street was now solid with women. Every woman out and

I had to walk through them. So I did. They parted for me. Then they began to spit. They spat on me so that my uniform, equipment, face, neck—even my hands—were covered in it. They spat while I marched through them, from in front, behind, both sides. In their hatred they spat upon each other. They spat in my eyes so I was nearly blind with the stuff.

When I got back I burned the uniform. I scrubbed. I thought about the stuff on my own mouth, some of it got inside. I was sick.

That night, thinking about Frank, it came to me I was privileged in a sense. I had an inkling, at first hand, what it felt like to be a European Jew in the high heydays of the thousand year Reich. To be hated. To be utterly outcast. To be spat upon and reviled.

BUT —— I had a hot shower to go back to. I carried a Sterling and a little yellow card that told me clearly when it was legal for me to press the trigger. So in another sense, whether I liked it or not—and I did not—*I understood what it was like to be a member of the Waffen SS*. This was hard to stomach. Whatever the objective truth of the matter if there is such a thing— those women, those children regarded me with the same loathing, the same self-righteous certainty of the just cause, the same conviction that I was sub-human and fit only to be destroyed that sustained the Underground in Europe and every liberation movement since. And I thought much the same of them when the blood was up.

I had served in Cyprus both in the back-shooting times and with the UN forces. None of this was new to me—except it *was*— because these Ulster Irish were in some sense my own people.

That was part of my understanding. It did not come all at once, neatly, as I have described it. It began long ago.

The Berlin days are blurred together. There is a scrappy journal in a war department exercise book (stolen) with entries in indelible pencil (stolen) one or two letters and, more important, a rack of books bought for me by Frank, mainly Penguins, from a book shop on the Ku-damm where they carried a big section of books in English. Nothing is written in the books but the feel of them in the hand, the places where the pages fall open, the pencil marks in the margins, these are more powerful reminders than any diary. Also the smell of them. The slight smell of age and the fading where the sun has caught sections of the orange covers. These things are evocative.

I have only to hold *The Good Soldier* to hear him say, "I treasure this, it should suit you, my dear corporal—try to catch him out."

"How?'

"Does he cheat? No he doesn't, the last mystery resolved on the last page. It is beautiful how it works, how it feels; but we'll talk about it, talk about it—poor Ford whom Hemingway hated because you always hate those you harm—a cruel brute, Hemingway. What the hell's the use of courage if you're a bloody monster. Grace in adversity, indeed. I prefer the small braveries of cowards. Anyway all those sort of terms of reference are *over*."

If I pick up *The Death of the Heart*, it is his own copy in grey slightly distorted hard covers I can hear him shouting at me in anger, "What do you mean you don't read books like this? Give me one respectable reason. I can understand if you tell me that the world these people inhabit is so alien to you that you cannot make any contact because they are *unreal*—if that is so then I will take you into that world. But the emotions, the passions, these surely you can understand. And if the worst comes to the worst use a bloody dictionary."

Editions Poetry, London (Nicholson and Watson) 1945. Not tattered exactly, but worn at the turn of the page: *By Grand Central Station I Sat Down and Wept.*

"This will break your heart, corporal, if you have a heart; this is what love means to a woman, and her man was also homosexual; it is time to broach the subject—and is she Jewish? I don't know but look at the way she interpolates the 'Song of Songs' into her private martyrdom. It is superb and self conscious and most marvellously *arranged*—tricky, very tricky the style she uses. How I admire her. Here, take it, keep it for me for a while."

And when I admit to him how much this world of books means to me ——

"Do you know what temptation really is, Jack? Do you know what Faust is really about for the artist? Fill my life with glorious

23

bursting ideas, unending ideas enough to make me wild with excitement because not even sex exceeds the orgasm of new discoveries. Inspire me and you can collect at midnight, December thirty-first, nineteen eighty-three, just to be on the safe side. That's the drug, oh excellent Mephistopheles, and you can shut Helen of Troy back in the sarcophagus."

"Did I tell you the title of my *opus*?"

"No Frank."

"*Juda Verrecka.*"

"What's that?"

He jumped up and made the Nazi salute. His face opened the way an ape snarls with the lips drawn hard back over the teeth. He shouted "Juda Verrecka" five or six times on a rising note and was almost foaming. Jack wondered if he was having a fit. Jack thought it was a bit comic but when he laughed it was from nerves.

Frank started to cough from the effort. He took a drink.

"It means Jews drop dead," he said. "I learned it in the Hitler Youth. The Ha-Jot as we affectionately called it. There I was in 1938 beavering away like, say, an earnest boy scout in England. But instead of lighting camp fires we used to flambé the local synagogue in the best petrol.

"And how, I hear you ask, could a little Jewish boy belong to the Ha-Jot—I will tell you if you will sit down and stop twitching. I had a non Jewish forebear. A gentile, a positive aryan. He put my Jewish grandmother in the family way in the middle of a field in high summer. It is not everyone who has so precise a knowledge of where a family keel was laid. So my mother was illegitimate, because the lusty lad went off to the colonies and never came back. But, but, but—years after, his brother . . . oh I really can't go into all that! Eventually—on that side of the family there were some poor but honest second cousins and when the heat was on, my mother in hiding and on the move from one comrade to the next, and my father was raising the money to bribe us out of the Third Reich, I was left with these people. They were stupid, ignorant and surprisingly filthy. They loved Hitler and like their children I joined the Hitler Youth and put on my little uniform and chanted Juda Verrecka with my little shoes crunching the broken glass on the pavement and my little heart full of a violent excitement and bestiality. I had ringworm I remember."

He sat down and scratched his head.

"Cropped," he said, "to the skull. Quite frankly they could have cut my balls off as long as they went on accepting me as one of the family."

It reminded him of something else.

"She often left me with strangers, the Cause came first you see! I was used to it; that's a lie—I never was. Sometimes she forgot to pay or ran out of money. They would speak of it in front of me. Sometimes I would be waiting to be collected. With my case packed. There was one place, a school, it was a holiday. All the others left. I stood all day in the hall. From after breakfast until nightfall. I would not move. I could not move. I held my case most of the time. They didn't want to give me any more meals. There was a window where I could just see the road. I felt that I must not leave that position or she would come and go again at once. I wet myself in the afternoon.

"When I heard her talk as she always did of the Cause, of suffering humanity—I was unconvinced! I knew from my cradle how much the Party cares. Omelettes and eggs they speak of quite often don't they?"

"But your father?"

"A sort of wraith in my memory. I suppose he had to choose. Her or me. She led a desperate life because she was a Trotskyite, my dear fellow—she never stood a chance once the purges started in Mother Russia. Not a chance —— here, read this man, where is he?—where the devil?... just a minute in the bedroom under the, the..."

The voice continues from the bedroom.

"... no good, no good to you, it's in French; anyway remember the name Serge, Victor Serge, he justifies a lot of the bloody misery; uncorruptible like my mother; I've spent half a life time trying to understand and of course they got her ——"

"Who?" I shout. If only I knew the terms of reference. If only there were even *photographs* to give me some reality.

"The Gestapo because she wouldn't get out with my father and me. The great Jewish net spent millions, you know, bribing a way out—but not her —— what were we talking about? Oh yes! I know! It all ties up as it usually does in the end—the ironic title

25

of my book *Jews Drop Dead*. I can see it in gold capital letters on a rich blue cover."

He was opening bottles of beer from the refrigerator and pouring on the slant two at the same time and already looking round for peanuts or bits to cram in his mouth and chew while he drank while he smoked while he talked.

"Do you know what a writer must do if he is not a genius? He must imitate and then find his own way afterwards. Unashamedly I will do that. You see I am going to write the Jewish *Catch 22*. The great Heller is my master. I am going to make a joke of the concentration camp. A most serious, terrible joke. I shall return again, and again, and again to some unspeakable horror at the centre. But I shall never describe it. I won't have to will I?"

His book, of which he never wrote a line, was remarkable. During the time in Berlin when he believed in it and believed in himself he told it to me.

The following statement was to be printed on the first blank page after the title page.

Early in 1933 Herr Goebbels issued a decree that all Jews were to be boycotted for a month throughout the Third Reich. In one remote German town after an exhaustive search they could not find a single Jewish citizen. The Burgermeister dispatched an urgent telegram to the Propaganda Minister. It read: *Send us a Jew for our boycott.*

The book began with the arrival of the solitary Jew, a flautist, at the railway station of the town on 31 March. There he was met by the official boycotting committee and the town band lined up on the platform. The band struck up an offensive song composed for the occasion and the children of the Ha-Jot (all volunteers at this time) unfurled a long banner which drooped in the middle. On it was written "WELCOME THE JEW SWINE". They also sang the disgusting words of the song. The sun shone on gold party badges and there was a feeling of carnival as the Jew stepped forward carrying his little flute case in one hand and his basket of kosher food in the other.

He stopped before the Burgermeister, stood to attention, and then, as the law prescribed, said firmly but with his eyes cast down, *"Ich bin der Juda..."* and gave his name.

The procession from the station began. The Jew was required to march at the very head of the column, before the band; rather as in other places and other days the Corn King went high-stepping to his dismemberment, to his fertilizing destiny.

This Jew, most surprisingly, handed his basket to a small boy, took his flute from its case and ...

And everyone that Frank had ever known as a child in Germany came tumbling after. His murdered mother, his dead father, his relations, Jewish, part Jewish and non Jewish; people glimpsed through the cracks of doors; over landings, running down the turn of stairs dizzy with sleep and fear; from windows in trains and trams—a world of characters transmuted to gothic proportions it seemed to me: giants, witches, shining heroes who sacrificed themselves; demonic killers. Many died, some endured to buy their way to Australia, Canada, America, Palestine even, passing through the eye of a needle named Lisbon.

When the real flesh-blood survivors of his past, the prototypes of these legendary characters who filled the unwritten pages of his book came to the flat it was a shock. After the witty and drunken and humane and wild outbursts filling my imagination, these people seemed a little two dimensional.

With the exception of Aunt Renata.

"In another time she would have been a patron of artists, of writers," said Frank.

She had a fine, hollow-cheeked face with a nose like an eagle's beak and deep lines in her skin as if she had been engraved. Her hair, shining black was full of gunmetal grey and scraped back round her head. The head was shaped to make you want to put your hands round it as you would a sculpture for the *satisfaction.* The eyes were large and under them such bruised patches you might have thought her desperately ill.

She was not ill. But she smoked every moment. Her voice was both musical and rasping.

"The sort of patron," said Frank, "who will combine the artist's mother, his sister, his mistress, his wife. He can run the gamut with her: incest, adultery. Suffer from passion, practise fidelity, discover that he must risk destruction even be destroyed by this liaison, by this fearsome combination of sexuality, intellect, flair and, on her part as well as his, savage self seeking."

All Jack knew was that she was the same age as his mother but her presence and her marvellous legs affected him sexually and made him ashamed of himself. She was larger than any life he had met previously. Also she frightened him.

I said that the Berlin days ran together. But I remember, quite clearly, that Sunday. It was the first time Aunt Renata paid any attention to me. Trigger number three.

It was very cold but fine. A steam out of the nostrils day. A morning full of heavy, well-wrapped Germans.

In the interval of the concert she said, "Well do you like it?"

The way she put a question made me feel my promotion depended on the answer. I looked round for Frank but he was away a moment. We were promenading upon a marble floor under the busts of dead composers, I suppose they were. Germans take a lot of exercise when they go to concerts or the opera. The audience was nearly all on the march. Nothing disorderly of course. More a parade. They spoke earnestly. Aunt Renata was bored for a moment because she had been pitching into Frank in German and somehow he had eased away.

"Not much."

"Ah! Why do you stay?"

"It is supposed to be good."

"Ah! And who says it is good?"

"Frank."

"Frank!"

"Yes, he says I have to stick it, listening to this sort of music, and then I'll grow to love it."

Jack failed to make the joke of it that Frank had done. Jack could not own up to the snobbish part—that if the intellectuals like Frank loved it then he *must* find out how to love it too, even if he hated it, really.

I laughed to show it was a joke but that I meant it. She did not laugh. She saw straight through me. No, worse—she saw there was nothing to see.

"Frank's opinion impresses you?"

"Yes it does as a matter of fact."

"And I suppose," she said lifting a hand and indicating the solemn audience on the march, "all these people, all these good people and their applause." She slightly stressed the word "good".

When she said it I realized that indeed they did impress me. More than that—I impressed myself to be among them, being careful not to clap at the wrong time.

"Yes," said Jack, "yes that's true."

Some people might have lied to Aunt Renata. Jack would rather have lied to the drill pig sergeant who made life almost unbearable in the first year of the boys' service.

"And," she said, "I imagine that the size of the orchestra, the volume of sound, the sense of occasion and disciplined dedication to culture and to the great Beethoven makes you feel in awe—as if you were in church perhaps?"

"No. It's too loud and it hurts."

She laughed. "What an honest boy!"

She took off her gloves. She held her hands out to me. First the backs of them and then palms up.

Her hands were far worse than my mother's. They were calloused, rough, the nails short, one or two broken. They were scrubbed, but the thickened skin on the working surfaces was not quite clean because of dirt deeply ingrained in it. The hands were very strong, masculine and out of proportion. In the second that Jack looked at them he felt them round his throat.

"I speak five languages," she said. "I knew the teachings of Freud *before* 1914, failed Rabbi that he was, he and Marx, my God, no wonder the Jews are ... never mind. I can tell you with authority this is a bad performance by an orchestra that should remain chained in the pit of the Opera House where no one notices the difference as long as the singers ... never mind."

She stopped, looked round her, took my arm. There was a frisson when she touched me. "Do you think it important that I know what I know? That I am, or was, an intellectual? You can't answer—never mind. Understand this—what is important, what really matters, as you will have seen by my hands is that I am strong. For over fourteen years now I have done jobs that an illiterate could do. Scrubbed floors, washed dishes and, most of all, cooked in a not very good restaurant. Long hours. Usually everything I wear and my skin and my hair smell of it—never mind. I do this because for a time I starved and my family starved. That is to say I do not have to do it—but I *must* do it."

She had an accent to her English which made what she said more emphatic than the words on paper can convey. When she spoke of starving, when she said "*must*", it conveyed the feeliing of starvation, the drive of the compulsion in a way that was quite total. It was this authority which so impressed me. As Jack used to say—she had been there.

She looked sideways at me, knew my feelings and said, "Ah! you are not just a clean, young English boy! Not just cricket and beer, is it? That is why he likes you even though you are not . . . never mind. What I am saying is that to understand why a work is a classic, even to love it because it is a classic—is merely a luxury. Do not let Frank mislead you. He believes, despite everything that has happened in his life, that culture is civilizing. It is not. I repeat it is not. Because of this he suffers. He is not able to understand what is essential to be civilized and what is a luxury."

"What is?" I asked, "what is? I mean I thought books and music and painting and the ideas, the visions you get. I mean —what it does for me in contrast to the army life—I mean."

I felt particularly stupid. I knew at that time I was like someone who understands more of a foreign language than he can speak. Jack seemed to understand the long monologues when Frank was in flood but it was more a question of feeling.

"Everything bad happens gradually," she said. "One little step at a time. Have you heard of pastor Neimoller?"

"No."

"It is not a crime, don't look depressed. He was a Christian here in Germany. He said something like this—that when the Nazis attacked the Communists (I mean the German Communists, you understand, this was in the early days of Hitler) he was a little uneasy but, after all, he was not a Communist! And when they attacked the Jews he was a little *more* uneasy but after all, he was not a Jew was he? Then the Nazis attacked the church, his church. He did something. It was too late, far too late."

The audience solemnly marched round. She watched them for a moment.

I could not work out if she hated them or had no feelings about them. She was still holding my arm. She disengaged sharply and took my programme from my hand; then a pen from her handbag, and rested the programme on a stair rail to write in it. It was a deliberate action and I thought of a treaty being signed or some formal declaration.

"There are two maxims," she said, "two great maxims, *Principiis obsta* and *Fines respice*. I have written them beside the name of Beethoven so that you will remember."

She laughed at my serious expression. She had all her own teeth. Then she did a strange thing. She darted her head at me and kissed me on the cheek. Not so much an embrace as a glancing blow.

"It is all right, corporal," she said. "I have written the meanings beside the Latin. The first means 'Resist the beginnings'; that is to say the very beginnings when everyone says you are being absurd and alarmist. The second means 'Consider the ends'. That is most difficult to do. But you have to try, you see. So if you have to choose between *kultur* and saying 'no' you will remember our talk."

Frank said from behind her, "That is a false choice."

"No," she said sharply, "no, no, no because a nation is its culture. Where did the philosophical ideas come from in this land eh? Hegel, Wagner and his disgusting son and daughter-in-law. And look at the English. They are not cultured in your sense at all. But they are wonderful when it comes to saying 'no' isn't it?"

"As one barbarian to another," said Frank, drawling it, "shall we return to our seats and enjoy the music?"

"You," said Renata, "you, my dear nephew, are besotted—do you like that word? It was one of the first I ever learned when I was interned as an enemy alien by the barbarian English whom I love and hate at the same time—you are as besotted with culture as I am with cooking. God knows why, but it clouds your mind, my dear."

"Of course it does," said Frank, "how absolutely right you are; but I mean to say don't you think the Jewish question is rather a bore? Hmm? Much better to curl up with a good book."

"I have to talk to you seriously."

"Not here I hope. Come we must go back."

"After the concert."

Frank said, "If you must," in a bored voice and then something in German.

Renata said in English, "One day you will get into trouble with your foolishness." She was distressed. Jack pretended not to see.

THE DERELICT TOWN.

What was he doing here? To whom did he talk? It is beyond belief that he was solitary.

I turn my back on the site of the burned house. The last time I spoke to him was three years ago; a day in London at the end of my first Ulster tour; a leaden, baking June day—and he had changed. Or perhaps I had changed.

I put my hands deep in my pockets, hunch into my overcoat, try to remember. Round me fences bulge outwards, grass forces up between granite setts brought a century ago from Aberdeen in coasters; weeds like young trees overhang breached walls and yellow dust from shattered bricks powders the dark earth and the turds of abandoned mongrels. Some of them lope by inviting the boot.

Hay fever, that was it. He had hay fever. He always had it in June. He was red in the face under the usual stubble and his eyes were swollen. The wine seemed to affect him more quickly than it used to. His speech was slurred. I do not know what foolishness Aunt Renata meant at that long-ago concert, but he was certainly in trouble that day in London. He was speaking of himself and Beatrice. He could not possibly have invented it. Nor would he. He never spoke with malice or fantasy of his adopted family. Jonathan and Beatrice were sacred—but yesterday when I saw her she seemed indifferent. Will Jonathan resolve it today? Will he come here to this derelict place to face me?

Speaking of Beatrice? Yes! I can hear him clearly as I stand here with the wind chewing at my face.

"If I ever found anyone like her, even a little like her, I would marry her, Jack."

"Marry *her* if you feel like that."

Nervous puff puff puff on the cigarette dropping ash on the plate before the waiter can clear it.

"The taboo is stronger than you think."

Outside the restaurant window, aching feet on the hot pavement tourists putt putt putting their breath against the menu as they converted the prices to dollars.

The taboo was incest. But it was not that. You cannot adopt incest! What other impediment to the unlikely union of Frank (ex-poof at the piano I remind myself) and Beatrice? The political business of Beatrice and her new friend about whom he was so bitter? I thought so that day. After seeing them, Beatrice and Peter together, yesterday—I still think so. And I am in a dangerous position now. Will Jonathan advise them to bring charges? Not if he is wise.

Roll on Jonathan—and what to do until he arrives?

I revolve slowly on my heels. Cars that had grilles like the teeth of Japanese generals and curves like the hips of belly dancers crouch on their wheel hubs with the last splinters of glass glinting in their split seats. They weather like sculptures, like shrines to dead Gods, into the ghostscape.

All colours around me are muted and English. Soft greys in which pigeons disappear; garden earth, brown as brushed suede; ochres and the red of old flower pots; green to rest your eye on: everything rain washed, windscoured, sea mist pitted; nothing half so garish as a red coat or the sun upon a chestful of medals and ribbons.

Old ladies and one or two male scarecrows are on the move. They drift through the alleys. Like tired ants they move to and from the single source of food and mutual comfort: a shack shop, shingled roof and leaning. On its wall in faded Victorian lettering the name of the demolished street. Opposite a crumbling hotel its window glass engraved with flowing patterns and the names of beers no longer brewed. Somewhere there are children. I hear their voices. I amble towards the shop which has no sign and linger outside the single plate-glass window.

Here is the listening post.

Here is the gossip centre. Frank must have used the place. I see through the smeared glass the goods stacked everywhere upon the floor inside. The ancient customers negotiate the waist-high cardboard boxes to approach the back where it is gloomy and I cannot make out the person serving.

I enter to the sound of the bell on a twist of flat metal

34

drowning the yells of children, the screech of diving gulls. The tops of old ladies turn to look at me as I negotiate white bread, lavatory rolls, toothpaste, soap, stale eggs, vegetables, ballpoint pens and dun-coloured cakes with white shreds embedded in them. I reach a single revolving stand of paperback books. It will do. I attempt to revolve it but it refuses. The sun of past summers has faded the bright covers. I look across the shop.

I see the woman for the first time. She is serving. She welcomes them by name as if they are members of her family. She laughs like a barmaid, full throated. A sound to make you laugh back at her. She seems to care about them. She seems to adjust to the mood—but the distortion begins here. To pretend that I re-create the circumstances of that day, in the moment before we spoke to each other, is false.

I am now so much part of the woman and she of me that her feelings, her vision, her sense of the place affects everything I say of it. She loves it and it draws her back. In the only real sense that matters I recognized her at once. And she me. We learn later, not much later, that we are both the children of ignorant, but loving parents and have each emancipated ourselves because there was something in us that forced us to it. We are dark and fair.

I buy a paperback without looking at the title. I leave it on the counter with the change after gossip. Genuinely forget it. Or so I believe. In the afternoon when it is nearly as dark as night she brings it to the hotel. To my room. We are alone in that strange, surviving inn. Two of us on the third floor and somewhere below the proprietors privately asleep in an over-heated room with a television set and a cat and glass-topped cocktail cabinet painted orange and green. She opens her arms to me.

Jack lies naked with the sheet between his legs. It is warm and drowsy. He speaks to her of his parents. He is uneasy. If he tells his story as Frank told him *Juda Verrecka* will it never be written because like *Juda Verrecka* it has been talked away?

It is inevitable that he tells her. He understands as he speaks that what happened to his parents—the indifference of the authorities, the shock and rage on his part—prepared him to see

35

the worst in Frank's death when, almost immediately afterwards, that news came to him. Only two months ago.

He tells her that Jack was a butcher's boy when he was fourteen. In the deadly boring village. That Jack was more stupid than his younger brother was never in doubt. More stupid and therefore more literal about any idea that penetrated his head. His mother worried about them both. She worried about many things and took a drink for it. You could smell it on her coming home from school. Not a bad smell because she cleaned her teeth to hide it. Peppermint alcohol in the air, bread and jam on the table, strong tea.

"Tea?" says the woman. Her name is Gwen. She is smiling. "Did you say tea?" She lies naked by Jack on the large bed in the hotel room. She is beautiful to look upon. Her legs are long. She lies with one knee bent her legs apart so that Jack may look down at her and enjoy her. Her breasts are soft, not large, and her nipples small and darkish in the twilight. She can lie uncovered and naked in comfort because the gas radiators are on and hissing and the wooden shutters are closed to a small gap at the tight shut windows.

"Shall I go down and ask for tea?"

"Not yet. Talk to me. Go on talking to me."

He tells her that his brother Ben demonstrated his independent intelligence by biting the school dentist and kicking the school doctor. It offended him to have probes and needles stuck in him. Later Ben went to grammar school which pleased his mum very much but worried her about the money for school uniform and fares. She had to take in stuff to sew. A woman came round about once a fortnight with a van to collect the finished stuff and leave. more to do. Jack did not like the woman. Ben did not notice the woman because of his homework. Sometimes the old sewing machine seemed red hot and Vera got backache. Charlie, sometimes called Chasser by his mates, was the father of Jack and Ben and played with them more than most dads when they were young. Tattooed on his right forearm was a heart and inside, bold as the needle could make it, was the name Vera. It was one of the ways he was identified when the fire brigade pulled them both out of the wreckage.

"Oh no."

"Sure."

The woman is upset and says, "Why do you say it like that? It sounds cruel."

"I'm not over it."

"Oh?"

"I think it's one of the reasons I came here."

"I don't understand."

"Nor do I. I think another reason was to meet you."

Vera told people that Jack was a good-looking little boy but too anxious like her. Too concerned with the problems of the family and not doing well at school. Jack got very upset in games when the rules were broken. He had fights and the headmaster sent for Vera and spoke to her about it. Vera knew that the headmaster did not understand and she herself could not find the words to explain. Nor can Jack even now. Why should an ignorant, village boy have a passion for justice. For fair play. For order? And his parents——

"What happened?"

"They went over a cliff a couple of months ago."

They were on holiday. Charlie and Vera on the spree for a cheap week late in the season. It was rotten weather but they made the best of it. I know because I went to the boarding house and asked about them.

"I'm ever so sorry, dear, about your mum and dad. We were ever so shocked, Timmy and me, we couldn't believe it; you're in the army aren't you, they talked about you?"

"Yes."

"Timmy was in the army, he was a driver. Look I put all their things together so you could see when you come; I suppose you got special leave?"

"Yes."

"It must be terrible over there in Ireland. I think they should bring you all home and let them get on with it."

"So do we."

They had a room up under the roof with a sloping ceiling. The wallpaper was very bright with yellow blotches; the bedcover was candlewick and pale green. The smell of all the cooking for days collected up there and lingered. Their toothbrushes were side by side in the plastic tumbler on the little glass shelf. I dropped them in the little tin waste bin, bronze with a black galleon on it.

"Were they happy?"

"Happy? Oh very happy, dear. They said they'd come again next year, they liked it ever so much despite the weather. People *are* coming back to us dear, not going abroad the way they used to when it was cheap—oh no! those days are over. They were a lovely old couple, they liked my cooking and the colour telly we got downstairs; did you see when you came in?"

"Yes, it's big."

"It's the biggest."

"Yes, I could see that."

She had the two suitcases open on the bed and was packing, briskly, ostentatiously; letting me see, as if I had by some psychic means an inventory of the things they left, that nothing was missing.

"They danced, you know."

She caught my expression and said, "They *did*! We have a knees-up after supper in the basement two or three nights. We got a piano down there and Timmy plays."

"Ah!"

"And," she said, closing the first lid, "they loved the dolphins."

"Dolphins?"

"Yes dear, real dolphins. They loved them. At the Dolphinarium."

There were three dolphins, two fully grown and one smaller, a sort of apprentice dolphin. They enjoyed themselves in the green water. The girl trainer wore white trousers and stood on a platform over the edge of the pool. She had nets and balls and buckets of fish. The dolphins loved her. They zipped under the water, leapt in shining arcs catching the lights, hit balls with their noses, turned somersaults, took fish from her mouth, landed sometimes with a tremendous splash that would have soaked five rows of spectators had there been any other than me. The white trousers got wet enough to show the pubic hair.

When the show was over the dolphins rushed the platform, flopped up on to it on their bellies honking for the last of the fish. The apprentice dolphin couldn't last out of the water as long as

38

the veterans. It was warm and humid. The water was jade making a green glow waver along the walls. The dolphins went back in and circled and circled. The lights went out except a working bulb. Round they went. Round and round and round until the next show. Round and round and round until it was time to die.

What to do?

A friend of my dad sold him the car. I had been to see him. I told him they were both dead because the car went over. He got angry and said, "Don't blame me. Nothin' to do with me, Jack."

His television was on in the background of the room. He was eating his supper off a tray watching the early news. It was bad news. Not as bad as my standing there saying, "It wasn't fit for the road". He did not reply. He sat there not looking at me, looking at the television. He stopped eating. He was about my dad's age, biggish, short of breath from smoking, the place was full of the smell of it. A milkman who went to bed early because he had to get up at five. Selling a few cars on the side to make a little.

He said suddenly, "The police didn't say anythin' did they? Nothin'—nor the coroner, I know that. It wasn't my fault, he should of kept it serviced I told him when I saw him which wasn't offen."

He was getting angry, raising his voice.

"He was your friend, wasn't he?"

"What you talkin' about? Who said he wasn't? What you doin'? Lookin' for trouble, Jack? You're not in Belfast now you know? You can't put the boot in here you know."

"The brakes failed."

"His bloody fault, then."

He was right about the police, they took it as routine. He was right about the coroner.

"But he was your friend," I said, keeping my hands off him, "he was your friend, your mate, your buddy—old buddy."

"You keep off."

"He used to get over here when he could, he used to give you things for the deep freeze—he trusted you, you bastard."

"Don't you use that tone with me, mate!"

"Friend, you were. You didn't even send a wreath with lies on the card, old friend."

His wife came in at the rush. She stood in front of him. She would not look at me.

"It's all right, Jessie," he said, "I can handle this don't you worry—I mean, I'll just get the police if I have to, won't I?"

She took her horrible dyed hair and her horrible slab of a face back to the kitchen.

He became dignified. He stood tall.

"Jack," he said, "men have to lead their own lives. I couldn't have got your dad to look after that car properly. You can't interfere with people, that's my motto."

There was a bird loose in the room. A budgie. Its cage was open and it flew round not interfering in anybody's life. It got its little claws into the curtains and hung there for a moment. It shat a thin stream on the carpet and my dad's friend smiled all over his face and said, "Naughty boy! You are a naughty boy, Chirpy, I'll have to put you back in your cage in a minute and you won't like that will you?" He said it in a fond voice and his eyes shone with affection.

I reached out and took the bird in my hand. It was soft and I could feel the small pump beating in it. I let its head come out between forefinger and middle finger.

"What you doin'?" he said.

"I'm going to kill it," I said.

"What?"

"I'm going to kill it."

He made a half-hearted lunge at me and then stopped as I lifted my hand with the bird as if to punch its head into the wall.

"You wouldn't do that Jack. You were always a good boy."

"Not any more," I said. "You know how it happened, do you, with that car?"

"Give us the bird, Jack, don't be silly now, I mean that's cruel —that's *bloody cruel*—Jack?"

"I worked it out," I said, "when they went over they had about five seconds before they hit. You count it; to get it right you count in thousands, like this: one thousand! two thousand!——"

"Don't hurt the bird."

". . . three thousand! four thousand!——"

40

"Jessie!" he yelled and she came rushing in from where she's been outside the door and they both raved at me and pleaded in the same breath.

"You wicked, cruel sod——"

"Please don't, poor little thing—please —— "

I took a punch at the wall and said, "Five thousand."

Jessie screamed.

I put the bird in its cage and shut the door.

"About five seconds," I said, "to know what was coming to them. It took the fire brigade two hours to get the remains out of the wreckage of that car you sold him."

But she was sitting in a chair gasping and crying and he was a bad colour trying to comfort her. The television set continued the bad news.

I went out through the door with the little stained glass windows in the top. When last seen the bird was pecking away at its sunflower seeds which should give it long life and happiness.

But what to do?

I had one day left of that compassionate leave. I picked the solicitor by the size of his brass plate. He was a small, fierce man. His forehead burned as if someone had put a hot iron on it. Drink. It was afternoon. He eyed me, suit and finger nails, as if I'd come for the job. I told him my story. He said leave it alone. I sat looking at him across his desk. He called me "sir" the way politicians and the police call you "sir".

There was a print on the wall beside him. A faded sea battle. There was a wasp at its last gasp butting the window pane. There was the smell of a bad cigar. There was the sound of a typewriter and stray traffic. It felt like the end of the world. I have been bored nearly to death, Christ knows, in the army at times—but this stale, empty moment did something to me.

Next time—if there ever was a next time—the police, the coroner and all other hollow pillars of society can do what they like: act with the scrupulous indifference which makes them fireproof. I shall settle my own business.

I know how easy it is. They do it in Belfast every day.

Warrant Officer, 2nd class, Jack reports back from compassionate leave after committing his parents to the furnace and not

41

collecting the ashes. Wreaths sent to local hospital which must cheer the patients who realize where they come from.

We were quartered in a warehouse converted to a fortress. Breeze blocks filled the windows. Out-thrust metal posts concreted into the tops of the outer walls carry barbed wire and metal screens. Chipped paint, concrete stairways, maps and naked women on the walls. Metal lockers, beer in cans, metal beds, formica-topped tables, metal showers, photographs of families. Echoing space under running boots.

I found two envelopes in my mail slot. In one was a letter from Ben, my brother, now in America. Why don't I buy myself out and join him? A coloured photograph of his family. He has not got fat yet.

In the other envelope was a cutting from the front page of an English provincial newspaper. A weekly. From a place on the coast where, I suddenly remembered, I was once taken in a school holiday. It was the first time in my life I saw the sea. It was wonderful. Ben and I both liked it so much we asked if we could live there. There was no inkling (it was the Festival of Britain summer, the new Elizabethan age!) that soon the small shipyard would close and the town begin to decay.

The cutting said that Frank died in a fire with another person, unknown, on the first floor of a condemned wooden house which he had rented a month or two earlier. A postmortem showed that both were drugged—or they might have noticed the fire and got out. The fire brigade had to come from the new town five miles away and took its time. This fact was elicited by Frank's adopted father referred to as "a London solicitor". It also reported that Beatrice was often in a state of collapse during the enquiry but had been the one to identify the body after the tragedy.

No wonder I could not contact him. I telephoned his flat three or four times the night I saw the dolphins. I stood in a lighted box on the empty seafront and dialled and dialled. Where the hell are you, I want to talk to you? It's been nearly three years. We did not part properly, openly, after that day in London. There was reservation, suspicion. At the other end the 'phone rang and rang. It was like the dolphins going round and round in the pool with the lights out.

I stood there, target in a lighted box. A National Front leaflet

42

was jammed behind the glass telling me how we could send all the coloured people in England safely home. And it was no big jump to remember Renata on Fascism. I turned in the box to look out over the dark sea at small bobbing lights where coasters lay up snug as they could get to avoid the coming gale from the south-west. The coloured lights of summer were out and over the concrete of the promenade the amber strips made it bleak as a frontier. Nothing moved.

I seemed to have spent my life waiting. You wait in the army, all right. That is the price. The 'phone kept ringing in his empty flat. I realized how like him I had become over the years. The influence of his presence when I was with him; of his letters because he wrote quite often. His desire for contact, no matter how tenuous, would see him at the typewriter, drunk, at three or four in the morning writing enormous letters without punctuation or capitals sometimes on lavatory paper to form a huge scroll— pink. Urging me to read, to think, to record. Sometimes maudlin. Sometimes obscene. Sometimes so delicately, so precisely, so wittily stated that I despaired—how could I ever in two lifetimes achieve such style? Those letters immediately changed the world. I mean literally. As one finished reading and looked up everything was different. Inspired! the corporal, later the sergeant, later the WO, went on an orgy of book buying, began yet another journal, disinterred the poems despaired of six months before. . . .

Writing this record it is easier by far to place him, indicate his tone of voice than my own. And yet the last time I met him I did not like him. It is hard to admit that. He was set one way and I another. It is hard to define. From the beginning I realized in a dim way that what sustained him, what he taught me, was the holiness of human genius, and the indestructible glory of the music, literature, art which flowed from it. He faced a world of which he had despaired by the time he was ten years old without recourse to any of the thousand faiths that man is heir to. Just reason and the uncompromising rejection of the second rate. No wonder he grew more lonely. In that sense only he was a rock. A rock from which a life-giving fountain burst, and the soldier drank. In every other way he was unreliable, often absurd and always elusive. He was also the best company you could have.

He once said, speaking of Aunt Renata, "We lose touch, perhaps we mean to. We drift. A little stab of guilt at Christmas or when some memory, some episode reminds us of the value of the other person. But usually there is something else isn't there? A block. With Renata, to tell you the truth, it seemed like a choice, I had to choose between her and Jonathan after Berlin."

"Between her *way* and Jonathan's," I said.

"Yes, if you like."

I sat on my bed in the fortress. I held the cutting and the envelope in my hand. The envelope was typed, correctly addressed, postmarked London. There was no covering letter.

What had made us drift apart? And on whose side? His or mine?

And who sent the cutting?

Jack tells the woman how Frank's view superimposed upon his own experience makes another sort of vision and out of that sometimes it is possible to write a poem. All his poems are about his village and the people there.

There was a tradition in Jack's part of England of going for a soldier. A hard tradition because it was that or starve in the cruel times and the cruel times were as late as the nineteen thirties. Charlie's elder brother Cyril went and he died of sunstroke in a camp in the desert in Egypt. They buried him by sunset the same day Charlie said. From his youngest days Jack heard these things mentioned and the ghosts of soldier boys redcoat and khaki marched the village street by night looking for their families long gone down the churchyard (they lock the church now against vandals, never needed to do that in the old days of the nineteen fifties).

Jack told Frank what it was like at home. Cesspit, get the rods out Charlie she's feeding back up again, ram it through and ring the council to come and pump out, the lazy buggers they don't care. Water butt brimming over with soft rain water to make the flowers and vegetables grow, should see it May June July the colours beautiful and the bees crawling over the blossom falling-over drunk with pollen and the big blue flies straight off the dog shit and in the kitchen past the plastic streamers to tramp over the bread, if you don't eat worse'n that before you die you'll be lucky, my lad.

44

Oil lamps in winter make a beautiful glow on the wall and light the lino on the floor, not one bit but five or six, oddments, Charlie picked them up at a sale, overlapping patterns blue and yellow and red and brown, checks and diamonds, colours dulled under the smear of boots. Vera is not too house proud, not got time to go on her benders and scrub got to keep the old sewing machine going make some money to keep Ben happy at grammar school. Poor old four-eyes Ben couldn't knock the skin off a rice pudding but let anyone lay a hand on him and . . .

Smells never noticed at the time from outdoor clothes worn year in year out, they don't have cleaners in a village not in those long-ago days of the forties and fifties; from washing on the boil the pong of piss out of pants sweat out of thick shirts going up in the steam staining the ceiling beading the window panes, get and hang it out Jack while there's a wind use the prop; from food in open pots on the cooker boiled fish vegetables joining the other smells and the lot driven out in spring when the door is open back and front by accident and the smell of the land comes through strong as an aphrodisiac, and then there's the smell of girls on fingers.

No books. Cats on a calendar. Old battery wireless. Dirty knees, snot under your nose. Charlie up at five summer and winter, sometimes earlier, to the lorry putting on or dragging off and folding the nail-ripping green tarpaulin, sodden wet most of the time, hard as a board when baked in midsummer sun, if you got that which wasn't often because the Bomb had changed the weather hadn't it and if it hadn't the Labour people had because Charlie was a Tory despite the cruel times when it was starve or go for a soldier. Charlie just missed them but his brother Cyril . . .

Frank told Jack that famous painters came to that part of England for two centuries. For the light for the mysterious shape of trees and the folds of landscape. For the windmills and the feeling of ancient times. For the witchcraft. Frank took Jack to galleries and showed him what at first he barely recognized—his own county. Frank talked of the lives of the painters . . .

But Frank would never know how it felt to lie tucked in the sagging bed close under the sloping roof and regard with wonder the patterns spread across it by the pretty shapes cut in the top of the valor oil stove. Safe safe safe. He was never safe all his days poor . . . old . . .

"Are you going to sleep?"

"No."

Jack lies on the hotel bed and listens to the hiss of the gas in the unsafe radiators. He does not want to burn. He knows the quickest way down, he checked last night. He prowled every inch of the place. The prepared line of retreat. If necessary out of the window and down on to the inn sign itself.

"Don't sleep, Jack."

He does not reply. For the first time in many months he is calm. He is surprised to find that he was not. Three deaths. But it is over. Something new will happen.

"I have to go soon, Jack."

"Why?"

"They all know me here."

"All!"

"Don't laugh."

"I love the smell of you. I love it."

"I want to believe what you say."

"When I first saw you in the shop today."

"It's only today, it is still today, it seems . . ."

"You immediately looked across at me like an old friend, I thought does she always? With every stranger? I wanted to believe . . ."

"No I don't always. I *don't*. I flirt, I know and I love people but when I saw you I felt like that, too. I know you. But I don't! It was very exciting. I wanted to ask you who you were straight away. It's this place as well. Because there are only a few of them left, the people, they are like wartime or something. They say *everything*. You catch it. I'm sure that's why I came this afternoon. It seemed the only reasonable thing to do! Reasonable! It was as if it was expected. I did not have to think. That's not true. I did think about it. But it seemed so natural. And I knew you wanted me to."

"Yes. Oh yes. But . . ."

"You think: do I do this every time a strange man comes to the place? Am I a tart? Am I desperate because I'm married and 30?"

46

"I'm desperate and I'm married and 36!"

"Ah! You do that don't you. You joke to hide, don't you?"

"Sometimes."

"And you do think that I . . .?"

"I wondered. You might."

"Didn't you care? I mean do you do it with everyone? Is it like that, Jack?"

"No. And I do care. I've been looking for you. But the past is over."

"I never have since I married. Not once. And I never meant to, either. Not because I didn't want to but because of the unhappiness it brings."

"Ah! you know about that?"

"There were plenty of married men before I was a married woman!"

"Ah!"

"Do you believe me?"

"All that matters is now. Like this. Trust it."

"You'll leave me."

"No I won't. It is already too late. Can't you see that, Gwen?"

"You say that but you will. All of them left me. The ones before I married."

"Not me."

"Why not. What's so special?"

"This. We are. Together."

—silence—

Now something is happening one or two floors below. Voices, a radio, and it is much later.

"I used to before I married. With anyone that asked. Except in business. I kept away from the ones in business. Except —— "

"Anyone?"

"Anyone I liked."

"No love?"

"Well, I thought each time—this one will marry me. I never took precautions."

"Kids?"

"No—how was I spared? Some of them stopped in time. Just some."

"I nearly came across to you this morning to take your hand —

47

I mean in the first moment I saw you. To take your hand and kiss your cheek like this—just brushing with my lips so I could feel the softness and smell the scent and perhaps your hair would touch my face. I wanted to trace the shape of your fingers, I love your hands, and encircle your wrist with thumb and finger, like this. Touch your palm with the tip of my tongue—then lean over you and look into your eyes to see the real colour—there, but not in this light! And look at your mouth close, close under me, in the kissing shape when you smile with the uneven teeth."

"They're not."

"They are. Yes, white and sharp to bite into my lip. I wanted to say very close to your ear closing my eyes in your hair, 'I'm Jack and I've been looking for you. I've come some awful croppers with women pretending to be you. I even married one to my shame because she suffers for it. I am a soldier by trade. I don't know why—it must be what I want or I wouldn't go on with it. I had a friend, a middle-aged Jew who looked no age at all except sometimes when his face fell into folds, terrible melancholy folds and he looked out from a kind of darkness like a pit and . . . but most of the time what you saw was the spirit of the man and that was ageless. Frank was his name and he died just up the road from here about two months ago. Did you know him?' "

"If you had I would have said, 'Yes I did, Jack'. He talked nineteen to the dozen except when I was talking twenty to the dozen and he made me laugh and I was terribly sorry when it happened although I wasn't here. At that time I only came down the odd three or four days to help out."

"Still in that shop I wanted to say as I took your hand and kissed your cheek, absolutely confident that you would like me to, I wanted to say 'But what are *you* doing here? the clothes, the scent you wear, the rings on your fingers, the beautiful sweep of your hair—who keeps you, lady, in this rich estate while you serve fags and bangers and swedes and carrots to these survivors who trek in and out?' "

"Touch me there again."

"Like this?"

"Yes. Yes. Oh I love this bed I love this room I love this light. Don't go away, don't go away."

"You are most beautiful."

"No! no!"

"To me you are beautiful."

"Like that, like that—oh God, Jack dearest Jack—but gently."

Light thrown up from the street lamp far below. Cars arriving, one or two, the bar is open down there. Long past tea time but she wants to hear of those he mistook for her down the years and he tells her about the first. Jack the fourteen-year-old butcher's boy riding the delivery bike with the big, wicker basket and the small front wheel fell in love with the girl who would not look at him. She was older. She laughed a lot, ran as fast as a boy, played football sometimes in the field that switchbacked with old mounds.

Bold girl who showed her knickers and had a boyfriend from the army, it was National Service days. The soldier was nineteen her brother Stanley told Jack, and he had a big one Stan said drawing it in chalk on the piss-house wall with two big danglers in the sack. He gave it to Stan's sister in the woods over by the army camp five miles away, she went there nights on her bike. Perhaps if Jack joined the army she would let him, too, when he came on leave, if he was a soldier boy and grew a big one.

Jack suffered a terrible, inarticulate anguish in his love and lust for the bold girl. He burned. Dumb Romeo butt and joke for Stan and the other lads; whisper and nudge as she goes flaunting by with her dark hair and eye, her easy swinging walk—we seen it, Jack, we seen it the other night, they do it on his coat, he puts her knickers in his pocket and you can see his arse going up and down and her making noises. Jack smashed big Stan in the face, went at him boot and fist, sent him running bleeding; found in himself the killer instinct.

So he joined as a boy soldier. Hated it the minute he was in. He tried to get out. Wrote a letter to his mum—fatch me back, spelled like that. But Charlie came all the way west to see him, driving the old lorry, God knows how he kept it on the road but he did. They went to a transport caff and over the fried egg and chips, sharing Charlie's fags the first time in his life—he still got a bit light headed when he sucked down the smoke—Charlie told him, you got to stick it out, Jack. In the war Charlie stayed a private the whole five years, never as much as made lance-jack; never complained, never volunteered. It'll get better, Jack, and

you chose it, you stick it now, boy, you do that. I'll take you back
to camp, now; you've grown a bit, stick up for yourself and shut
your mouth; your mum sent you this made it yesterday, says to
write when you can. Give you enough to eat do they? Keep your
nose clean you might end up a sergeant! Think o' that.

"Was she like me, that girl?"

"Yes."

"Looked like me?"

"I don't know. I think I've always been looking for the same
woman. I kept finding aspects of her. No one has looked as you
look."

"Your wife?"

"I thought so—I was wrong."

"Now me. Are you wrong again?"

"It is you. She is you. The one I have always had in my mind,
in my heart."

"How can you be sure?"

"Because I feel no guilt."

"Oh."

"Do you?"

"No—I'm terrified but I don't feel———."

"You see."

"Not really!"

"Well I feel it is inevitable no matter the cost."

—silence—

"I was like her when I was young."

"Who?"

"Your village girl. We did it out on the marshes. It was beautiful in the open. Beautiful the smell of everything around and the
gulls floating overhead, the sky behind his head. Do you mind
that?"

"No. Yes I do. I shall mind it more when you've gone; when
I can't touch you like this and know it's me and only me—because
it won't be will it?"

"It will take years to know you, Jack."

"And you, and you."

"I had given up all hope of this."

"Of course! That's part of it I realize; I never thought I'd
meet her now. I was sure it was too late and I know too much

50

—you can't be total when you know too much; but now I think I can. You are, she is, sensual and animal, understanding and subtle—you make me . . . you make everything possible again. For the first time since I was that yob, that thick-headed, red-faced lout suffering the pangs of unrequited passion! You make me."

"No it's you. It's you. I feel the same; just the same as when it was the marshes and I thought he'd marry me; like the first time I had an orgasm I was sixteen—but I'm jealous, why aren't you?"

"Of what?"

"Of everything I have never shared with you. Of your wife. I hate your wife. Don't laugh, don't laugh. I'm jealous of everything I don't know about you and I have only been with you a day! If you don't feel like that too you'll betray me."

"I won't let myself think of the things that make me violent. I am very violent sometimes, when it blows—so it is better not to think of your husband. Your world. Anyway the past is over. Really over. Now is reality for us. Choose and be grateful. You are she—and even so I may betray you both!"

"Don't laugh at me, don't."

"Are you special then?"

"Yes yes yes, let me go; I'll cover you with bites, I'll leave nail marks all over you. I'll brand you so that anyone seeing you will know!"

"And if I do to you?"

—silence—

"Will you betray me, Jack?"

"It's possible!"

"Are you doing it now? Have you been since I stripped for you?"

"What do you think?"

"I can't see you any more."

"I can see you. I have better night sight. You look slightly off the object."

"Object! I am holding the object so look out."

—silence—

"Will your husband come looking for you? Will I have to hide in the cupboard?"

"He's in London."

"For the day?"

"We live in London. I have a business there. I'm only doing the shop for my auntie while she's in hospital poor soul it's the veins in her legs!"

"Oh?"

"They're taking them out like long worms!"

"That's nice!"

"I love it here, coming back here, any excuse. It's all changing, going, ending. I hate that."

"I won't betray you, Gwen."

"That's nice when you say my name. We'll wear each other out, won't we?"

"No. We're not static people—we are like two springs. Don't question the source just trust that fresh water will flow and flow—why did you marry?"

"I wanted to be safe. There were too many men; too much using, picking up and dropping, it made me sick in the end. I wanted—to be safe."

"You're not safe any more, girl."

"No. I'm frightened again. And excited again. I want it to go on and on; I want it, I want it, I want it. Oh God that was a burden when I was young—Oh God."

"Don't cry. It's all right."

"The itch and the heat, being on heat and having it and thinking the minute it was over how soon will I have it again and none of them giving a damn and nor did I except I *did* because I thought they must love me really. Oh dear this will put you off, frighten you off, I'm not like it now but it is so beautiful making love with you."

"It excites me. It makes me feel tremendous."

"You excite me without touching me even."

"I couldn't keep it down this morning when I first saw you."

"I know. I looked. You had your coat open that's why you bought that book and held it in front of your flies."

"No it wasn't!"

"It *was*, and if it wasn't it should have been."

"I wanted you there and then, on the counter—don't laugh so *loud*!"

"Sorry."

"Your tears taste cold. Isn't that strange in this warm room? And not salt at all, they are supposed to be."

"Crying and laughing my goodness what must I look like, don't put on the light yet."

"I bet your laugh is known for twenty miles round here."

"Forty!"

—silence—

"Did you love him, your friend?"

"Yes."

"He was queer."

"And the rest!"

"Is he the reason you don't sound like a soldier? You look like one, and I ought to know!—but you don't sound."

"That's clever of you."

"I think you're like me. You've got two voices."

"Yes."

"The one I was born with here."

"I heard it in the shop today."

"And the one I picked up later."

"That's it. What do you do?"

"I design and make jewellery."

"Make?"

"Yes, workbench and all, soldier."

"I'd like to see that."

"I hope you will—your other voice is the poet is it?"

"I suppose so. I don't think about it, I just switch automatically to the one that suits. I'm a snob as well!"

"Only a poet would believe it—would love me and be mad enough to believe it could last forever or even to the day after tomorrow."

"I believe it."

"You will have to reassure me every day."

"Sometimes you will have to reassure me."

"You seem so certain."

"That's training."

—silence—

"I have just understood something. Due to you. Being with you. Being able to tell you. I can explain why I am here, I think. The heart of it."

53

"Stay like that."

"Am I too heavy?"

"No."

"Frank thought he was an artist. A writer. His life's work was to be his book. He became progressively more isolated because he never wrote it. So he thought himself a failed artist. He dabbled in other things, pirate records, arts programmes—but it was no good. What he really was, I realize, was an artist who did not understand his talents. His talent was to inspire. And no one will know if I don't tell them. I want to give him a memorial. To say that with one person at least he succeeded. I thought I might be here to avenge him. I may still. But I realize now that the other is what matters. I will write *Juda Verrecka* for him. Do you see?"

"How can I when I'm dazed with you and—I can't think of anything except us together and what will it be like tomorrow?"

"I adore you."

"Then you won't leave me."

"Yes. But I'll come back."

—silence—

"I'm terribly hungry."

"So am I."

"I want to cook for you."

"Not tonight. Tonight we'll eat downstairs bold as brass."

"I'm even jealous of your dead friend so watch out. Did you ever think that the woman when you found her might be violent —and cruel—and unreasonable—and everything that drives men off and frightens them—and that she might want it all—everything—and want it now—no concessions—and that she always told herself that some day someone would talk to her the way you do, and frighten her the way you do—and that she is a shrew half the time, and in a panic and cannot stop telling you, trying to make you go the moment you have arrived so that it will confirm her fears; but at least there is a chance you won't have broken her heart in such a short time? That's what it's like and I want to eat you—like this—and this. Oh God I never cry, I never cry —— isn't it silly I only came up here to give you your book and your change—I only wanted to talk a little. I have never felt like this—it's like drowning I never let anyone get to me, never!"

54

Now you've done it, Jack. Now you're in it. You thought all those sentimental years that when she finally turned up the woman would be beautiful like a spring day, full of light. Instead—a tornado; thunder, lightning, ideas torn up like trees; everything whirling in the air displaced. But how glorious after the first terror of the force of it to be awake at last. To open your arms to it. Everything is unknown and dangerous. She wants everything. So do you.

PART TWO

III

T HERE WAS A course we attended in plain clothes. In the country. Near a pub where you could play skittles. Where the grass was rich and green and the beer as chemical as everywhere else.

Officers and NCOs, mixed, sat at desks like school kids (Jack remembered the one-room school in his village where they went, all ages to ten-and-a-half, and the mistress came every day in a little Austin 7 that Chasser his dad put right for her when it wouldn't advance and retard or some such by-gone piece of engineering).

A blue bow tie and glasses; a very certain-of-himself gentleman up there.

"Is this a possible label for a political party? Marxist/Stalinist/ Maoist/International Socialist/Workers' Revolutionary/Solidarity Action and Liberation/Civil Rights DEMOCRATIC Campaign?

"Not possible, I'm sure I hear you say, because upon the Sino/ Russian frontier they raised a large picture of Mao, the Russians responded with a picture of Kruschev and the Chinese turned their backs and dropped their trousers and aimed their bare arses in a gesture unmistakable. So if the Russians defecate upon the moon face of Mao and the Chinese spew upon the Soviet Union—and they have even been known to shed some blood . . .?

"I will not keep you in suspense. There is one word, one name that links them all. Put that name instead of my exaggerated label and all is unity? Any guesses? It *is* rather warm this afternoon and out there the hum of innumerable bees, or something equally soporific, is bearing on your eyelids, perhaps we can open a window. Thank you.

"The name is Lenin.

"Where two or three are gathered together to raise clenched fists (meaning gentlemen it is their intention to bury you, sooner rather than later) and wherever proletarian or student or intellectual or parliamentary or artistic voices ring out upon the noonday air singing that they *'Will Overcome'* or they *'Will Not Be Moved'*, usually to the accompaniment of out-of-tune guitars—there the spirit of Lenin is celebrated.

"Be patient—I will come soon enough, as will this course of instruction, to the business of nail bombs, kneecapping, prepared lines of retreat for snipers, use of hostile crowds to prevent the wounded being cleared and the planting or stealing of weapons etcetera etcetera—most of which also stems from the explicit instructions of the great Lenin. I will spare you Churchill's immortal quote ——

"There is an illusion, fostered deliberately by some of your fellow citizens, and supported by numbers of others who are politically illiterate, some in parliament, some in trade unions, some in the media, some in the universities, that the Left is split.

"The combined party of Lenin is never split in that sense. Its strategy never changes. Only the tactics change. The last painful (for them) all-change was after Cuba. They had to *retreat!* They have made up for it since!

"Do not, therefore, be deluded by the protective colouring of those labels—Workers', Peoples' and so on, usually tacked on to the all-purpose lies-are-truth and black-is-white and war-is-peace magic word of our time—DEMOCRACY. Beware those who flourish it.

"Ignore the apparent schisms, the violent clashes as the Trots rail against lads of King Street and bear in mind that one and all they revere Lenin.

"Lenin is not mocked."

And on he went to practical matters shielded by the Official Secrets Act. To film clips, video tape, stills and diagrams. Members, overt and covert, sympathizers. Fronts, individuals and organizations.

Jack, drowsy, jerks awake.

Jesus Christ there's Edward I thought he was dead.

"How old is that picture, sir?"

"Why?"

"I've noticed one or two that seem out of date from the clothes."

"Excellent point. This one is—five years."

He *is* dead. The whisky must have got him in the end. Renata told me he was dead when I went to see her, but it was a shock to see him on the screen.

The bow tie speaks of the links between liberation movements. Which brings him to weapons. The way they get passed round. Who sells them. What we can expect.

(In the glove compartment of the car is a Luger automatic 7-65mm taken from the body of a rompered Prod. German source. Lifted by Jack.)

"But you won't win with weapons in the end. Consider the American experience in Vietnam." (He pronounces it Veetnam.) "They were stupid enough to ignore the French experience. You'll win with ideas. You'd better know what keeps them coming. You'd better know it's life and death. You'd better decide if the country you serve is worth the candle. If in doubt, shut your ears to the words, look hard at the actions. Try to get inside the skin of the man who loathes freedom! The man who finds the open society disgusting and repulsive. That should not be so difficult for you gentlemen. Numbers of you detest, for example, student demonstrations, long hair, the mockery of institutions—I mention it in case you are tempted to be holier than Lenin—which would hardly be possible —— do I hear the word tea?"

Berlin. At the time of the concert when Jack learned the meaning of *Principiis Obsta* and *Fines Respice* and *Juda Verrecka*.

Non-existent, like a servant in the great days of the Raj, he sat silent, and observed.

It was like watching a play. Most of them, when they spoke English, spoke what Jack thought of at that time as "officer" English. It made them seem more mysterious: the contrast between the English voice and the foreign gesture; the cut-glass accent coming out of biblical faces marked with suffering. Some were in education, others vaguely to do with music, opera, ballet.

English wraiths from the British Council and the Arts Council sometimes eased through a crack in the door to join the conversation.

In curious and wispy ways by hint and smile, by scrap of telephone conversation, by letter of introduction, by some network more sensed than stated they supported each other while they

61

tore each other to pieces—to weep, embrace and put the pieces together again with the glue of past horrors shared.

Emigrés they mostly were, come back to the hated, needed homeland.

By either her second or third husband, I am not sure which, Aunt Renata had a daughter who grew up with oversize breasts to strut upon stilt heels like a stroppy pigeon. She had red hair and wore aggressive spectacles. Her name was Rosa. Frank called her Beastly Bertha behind her back.

She was bi-lingual; spoke excellent English in the assertive, slightly hectoring, style of male interviewers in political television programmes and regularly talked Frank down. She was married to Edward, a middle-aged Englishman. Frank said that at least six others were knocking her off.

Rosa was a travesty of her mother. Forceful, without compassion. Strident, without self knowledge. Aggressive but incapable of selfless love, of sacrifice. Rosa was the power and the dogma.

Edward, in contrast, seldom opened the trap under the moustache. His hair was long for the time. It flowed past the ears and over the collar. He was Welsh so perhaps Lloyd George knew his mother. To show that he was acceptable, really, he wore a tweed jacket with leather cuffs and patches at the elbows and a tie that could have been from almost any unknown public school, and twill trousers. His shoes were always polished bright.

He had the officer voice but it was very soft. His nervous habit of rolling up his eyes to show the whites when stressing, or rather understressing, a point caused Frank to say that you could shoot anytime with those eyes.

The pair of them wangled a job in Berlin.

On the fringe of the emigrés was another group of Germans associated with them: university professors, writers, intellectuals and other relations of those who did not survive the heat of the fire. Some worked in the East zone. It was impossible to decide which were the sucker fish and which the sharks. Into this group Beastly Bertha and Edward faded and re-appeared and faded— Jack caught whispers of some trouble they left behind in England. Mystery, mystery.

*　　*　　*

We walked briskly away from the concert hall in the winter sun. She was between us holding an arm each. Frank had both hands shoved deep in his pockets and his head pulled into his collar. As usual he had not shaved thoroughly because he was probably making coffee reading a newspaper and trying to find his other shoe at the same time. The sun revealed unscythed tufts under the corner of the jaw.

Aunt Renata said again, "I have to speak of it—she is my daughter after all and Edward —— "

Frank said sharply, "I am not responsible for the mistake you made in early middle life, Renata—nor that they got themselves into trouble in the East."

It was pompous for him. She should have shut up.

"That is not the point, Frank," she said, "you lost your temper because you were caught with your friend —— "

"Caught," said Frank furiously, "caught—what are you talking about, did that cow say —— "

"The American," said Renata, "and I do not literally mean caught I mean the arrival of Edward and —— "

"At four in the morning," said Frank, "your daughter and that middle-aged consort that she married as some kind of a father substitute came ringing the bell at —— "

"There you are," said Renata, "it made you angry and you were unwise enough to say in front of Edward —— "

She was near one of the dangerous places in his mind. It seemed so obvious. In the face, in the eyes. Jack tried to divert him with a joke about some Germans going by, but Frank raised his voice to drown him and said, as if it were the point of the whole argument, "I was not angry to be 'caught' as you put it. I am homosexual and have never pretended otherwise—except on those occasions, mainly social, when it would have embarrassed my friends. I am, in fact, a perfect product of the English education system even if I did start late —— "

Renata stopped walking making us stop. She said very sharply, "Stop it! Stop it at once this exhibition."

We stood in a huddle as people went by. It was a shining, good-to-be-alive morning. A little further on flags were whipping and streaming high in the sharp air and over them a jet trailed the sky white against the winter blue.

We continued to stand because now Frank would not move on. Something had taken over. He looked at us but was not in our company. Renata, oblivious to this change in him which I had seen before, pressed further, "We are all the same family," she said and nearly put those frightening hands on him to shake him, "family, family—it is not that I *approve* of my daughter, but I fear for you, Frank."

He was still as a wax dummy. This passivity enraged her.

"Must I spell it to you," she hissed close to his face, "must I? Edward is still Stalinist, how could you be so stupid as to mention your mother in front of him."

As she said this Frank moved convulsively as if someone had put ice down his neck. Both his and Aunt Renata's behaviour was comic to look at. The situation made me nervous and I nearly laughed. The intensity, the incongruity.

In that moment he turned violently away jerking free of her and immediately tried to throw himself under the passing traffic. A parked van rather than Jack's reflexes saved him. He did not have time to get round it before Jack caught him.

No thought went into this. Instinct only. Frank tried to shake himself free. He was not strong but he had unusual strength at this moment. It was a scrabbling mess as Jack struggled to pin him. Jack did not want to hurt him, nor did he want them to be arrested, or for others to join in. He was aware of Renata's face, stern and unrelenting looking round to see who was nearby. Frank struck at him with a free hand hitting his face and Jack lost his temper.

People were stopping and looking now. It was not orderly to behave in this way—quite disorderly to dare to attempt to cross where there was no crossing—or was it a kidnapping to the other side? This happened. This, and tunnels, and murder out of fountain-pen guns. Jack held him still, locked with the arm up behind, nearly choking him with the other arm round his neck. It was violent and quick. Jack said into his ear, "I'll lay you out if I have to—I'll choke you till you drop do you hear?"

"Get off get off, I'll kill you, get off."

"Do you want to be arrested?"

"I don't care, you stupid, interfering prick."

"I care. I'm a soldier, they'll put me in the glasshouse."

64

Renata was beside them. She was very clever. Jack held him against the side of the van. She stood close to hide them as much as possible from people on one side.

"They've already sent a hard man to interrogate me," Jack said, "do you hear?"

She looked shocked but Frank just struggled. Jack tightened on his wind pipe, "About *you*, mate," he said, "you and your friends, how do you like that?"

"What a fool he is," said Aunt Renata, "let him kill himself. He is like his father. Look at him! Let him go I tell you."

I felt the purpose go out of him. Aunt Renata had timed it well.

"Interrogated?" he said for something to say, coughing through the word. I let go of him. He got a handkerchief, dirty of course, hawked and spat into it and stood dishevelled and miserable looking past us.

He said, "I would have welcomed it. All sense of self goes."

"Walk," said Aunt Renata with a bright smile on her face, "walk my dear boys the police are coming." We walked arm-in-arm as before. It was not the police, simply some stewards from an airline still in their uniforms. But Renata was talking to Frank in German, laughing and rebuking, even turning to me: it was a fine performance of a mother telling her sons not to play games in the street, to be their age and behave—even if it was one of their birthdays. She switched it on until we were comfortably away and then she switched it off. It was a reflex from other days.

They were both pale. Frank would not look at me. Aunt Renata said, "Is your face all right?"

"Yes."

"You did well, corporal."

Jack, embarrassed, used the barrack-room voice to excess. "Well he's my mate ent he? I ask you my bloody mate that gives me books and plays me music and thumps me in the mush, dunne the rotten sod?"

"Oh God," he said, "hearts an' flowers next."

"The hard man," said Jack, "was very nasty to me, Franky." He detested being called "Franky". "He said that I got friends that are poofs an' it'll all go in my service record unless I keep an eye on my poofy friends and tell 'im what they get up to! 'Ow

65

do yer like that, then, Franky, eh? 'E as good as said I'm an inverted pervert or nancy for short!"

"Oh Christ!" he said in despair, "how disgusting—how I loathe the time we live in. She," he indicated Aunt Renata, "believes that culture is a luxury and tells me every time we meet that men used to read Goethe in the evening, that they listened to Bach and Mozart by candlelight and then, in the morning, they went to work in Auschwitz. Do you know what this does to me? It poisons the very spring of humanity, it murders my faith in the unspeakable glories of genius, just as my mother was murdered for her faith in the ultimate *compassion* of the Marxist ideal. And now you," he said and he could hardly articulate, "my friend I believe, is to be my spy—has already been my spy—it is vile, vile and degenerate."

"Never mind," Jack said heartless as he could make it, "never mind, cock—I was the thickest idiot he ever interviewed. You know why?"

"No."

"They told us at school diden they eh?—you don't split on your mates. And what are you?"

It sank in for a moment, but he could not help saying, "Is it true?" He was thinking that in the reverse position he might well betray me.

"Cross my heart. Anyway what's wrong wiv books an' music an' you goin' on for hours? I mean if any of your friends started something that threatened Queen and Country I'd do somethin' about it even wivout that man pushing me wouldn't I Franky—now be fair?"

He started to laugh. "True blue," he said, "a proper little working-class Tory. And there he is," he said to Aunt Renata, "pronouncing the classic liberal E. M. Forster doctrine—about the choice between betraying friends and betraying country—well almost. I'm hungry are you hungry?"

Aunt Renata said, "Now you know why I was angry about what happened with Edward the other night—it's *dangerous* for you."

"No!" said Frank, "the truth is *you* can't bear anyone to rock the boat when it comes to family. But you do not spare *my* feelings."

"She was my sister," said Aunt Renata fiercely, "my sister as well as your mother, do you think I mention it lightly when I know how *I* still feel?"

"Oh shut up about it," said Frank, "shut up about it."

"The reason," said Aunt Renata actually shaking him from her side, "that Jack has been interrogated *is not you*. It is some of those who come by—it is Edward. There is a file on Edward."

That was too much for Frank. He literally threw up his hands in response, "A file on Edward," he said with scorn, "a *file* on *Edward*. For God's sake Renata spare us such imbecility. I don't expect from you the refugee paranoia." He turned to me and, knowing that half the time he did exactly the same thing himself, he was still able to say, "They go round and round and round whispering and backbiting, inventing, accusing to satisfy their fears and guilt—they are persecuted by persecution manias—but Edward! I mean, you have *seen* the unspeakable fart, haven't you."

"It is true," said Aunt Renata grimly, "when you are reasonable I will explain how I know. If you doubt me, then write to your adopted father ——— "

"Father," said Frank furiously because now he believed her and it was another blow to add to the bestiality that culture could not cure, to the friend who is an informer. "Jonathan *is* my father since I was ten or something so don't be a pedant."

"Your father," said Renata now equally angry and raising her voice for the first time, "your real father died of cancer which is to say of *shame* because you and he got out and your mother did not, he bought you out—Jonathan is your foster father, your adopted father—your *English* father if you like, but I will not call him your father."

She was ferociously angry. What about? After such iron control all the morning, after such care not to cause a scene.

We were near the place that Frank had pointed out on our first meeting to have been a Gestapo building of some kind.

It took the frightening force of her anger to stop him at last.

"I am sorry," he said, "I am sorry."

She would not reply.

"I know you loved my father," he said, "it came to me the

67

other night after the scene. It just surfaced. I'm sorry. Deeply sorry. Forgive me."

"You are a fool," she said, "he was a fool. And I loved him with all my heart. Now, at last, I have said it."

She turned on him with her arms wide and I was not sure if she was going to strike him. Instead she put her arms round him and pulled his head to her. For a moment he resisted then he stood there with his arms round her and wept without a trace of English shame.

I remember the taste of the soup. Thick and meaty and spicy and bubbling, and black bread with it, and frozen butter in yellow wedges showing teeth marks.

Jack made a note in the WD exercise book in indelible pencil which is now faded purple and spread like water colour. It told me to go to the restaurant where Aunt Renata worked when I was on leave in the Smoke because she was an ace cook. I meant to. For years I meant to.

Beatrice told me where to find her. In Balham.

She was in a wheelchair sitting bolt upright with a shawl round her shoulders and a grey blanket over her legs. Her hip was broken and would not mend. She had had a stroke in the night and fallen from the hospital bed where she lay with the metal pinned hip. No one noticed for some time. She spoke slowly, and to remember caused her great effort and pain. She was cold. She was cold out of proportion to the heat of the room where a gas fire burned and an upright oil stove. I sat before her in a sagging chair and she looked at me quite unblinking with her fine intelligent eyes. She looked into me and past me. There were long silences.

The light in the room was a bare bulb to save electricity by not wasting it with a shade. She owned the small terraced house. It was her one certainty on earth. Two walls of the room were full of books. On the table before the gas fire were photographs and mementos arranged as if on exhibition under glass.

The photograph of Frank's father and Renata's sister with the little dark boy was easy to identify.

I could not be sure of the irony when she indicated it and I handed it to her and she looked for some time through her glasses and said, "What a fine couple with their son—how I envied their future."

Her husband—was it her third husband?—came into the room with tea for us. He had never learned to speak adequate English. Clearly he did not like her. Perhaps he was punishing her for past deeds although usually it is women who do that, men are too lazy or lacking in purpose.

How do I know? Her hand shook although she tried to control it. In fact with this inner cold she shook slightly all the time. He gave her a mug of tea and another to me and also a biscuit to each of us but he provided no tray, no side table and left her with one in each hand.

She began to call him back. I looked round but could see nothing to put by her wheelchair. I stood by her and took the biscuit. She put both hands round the cup and drank carefully. He had heard and came back into the room. She asked him for another fire. He told her it was warm enough and spoke of the bill for heating. She accepted calmly.

When we were alone and the tea drunk she said, "You know Frank—loved—you—more—than—anyone?"

"No," I said, "I did not know, Aunt Renata."

"Oh yes," she said the words spaced carefully as she tried to breathe properly and was always a little short of air, "oh yes, it was because you were the only person he could trust completely, you see? He loved your trustworthiness because he knew he was not, I suppose. You did not judge him. Nor—did—you—desert—him."

"No," I said, "why should I?"

She became anxious and looked at me with hostility almost.

"You—are—in—the—army still?"

"Yes."

"Not the police?"

"No."

"Not—the—police?"

"No."

"Not some—spying—business?"

"No."

I did not ask why. I did not have to ask why.

69

I felt great pain to see what happened to such intelligence, such courage, such wit and style. It sat before me in a wheelchair having only dignity left. That was something.

She said, "There is something wrong."

I did not understand and began to ask if I could help her to be more comfortable, get another blanket. She moved her hand impatiently brushing me off like a fly.

"He did not," she said and stopped.

"Frank?"

She made the movement again because my stupid interruptions interfered with her forming the thought.

She said, "The—death—was—wrong—you—will—see."

My expression caught her eye. For a moment she smiled and it will sound excessive I suppose but as that happened I yearned to comfort and cure her but knew she would soon die.

(I drove that night to the place on the coast. I drove very carefully.)

"A good clean English boy," she said, "what a relief after . . ." and she made a flapping gesture with her hand that I have only seen in Europe. It implied the rest of her life. Not a bad joke to end on.

I said I would come again.

I remember the taste of the soup. I was starving because it was mid-afternoon before Renata dished it up.

"Aunt Renata," I said, "you are an ace cook."

"It is my vocation," she said, "to feed the hungry," and then she laughed the hoarse attractive laugh showing her strong teeth.

"So eat up, corporal."

"I shall write down the name of your restaurant."

"More a café," she said, "poor people eat there. There are even some poor Jews in England, you know!"

"I doubt it," said Frank gloomily, "I've never seen one."

She cuffed his head and said, "Go to Israel and work for a living."

"What!" he said. "Me go to Israel—give it two generations and the *German* Jews in Israel will run the whole outfit. And how will they run it?" He leapt up, clicked his heels, gave the Nazi salute and shouted "Zeig Heil!"

70

"Nonsense."

One of Frank's themes was that the German Jew was different from every other kind of Jew—and worse. The American boy friend said he was an anti-semitic Semite.

Frank said, "Well you had better tell me."

This abrupt change was not expected by Aunt Renata. She sat smoking a cigarette the empty soup dish in front of her. She did not immediately reply.

"I knew there was trouble of some sort," said Frank, "or Rosa and Edward would not have come here."

Beastly Bertha was Rosa after Rosa Luxembourg whom Aunt Renata revered. It was an unfortunate choice to associate the turgid daughter with the brilliant and fiery martyr of the Left—but even someone as clear eyed as Aunt Renata must have the comfort of a few illusions. It is that or go mad.

She was uneasy to speak in front of me. She could have told him in German, of course, but after the events of the day it would have seemed uncivil. We were very friendly and full of hot soup, after all.

I had not been there, of course, two nights before when Rosa and Edward intruded upon Frank. The physical result, two broken upright chairs and one broken occasional table, stood in a corner of the room waiting to be collected and repaired.

I remember the taste of the soup. I remember the smell of the cigarette Aunt Renata was smoking, an American cigarette. I feel the unusual silence into which we seemed to curl like cats into heat.

The atmosphere of that time laps round me; not so much the hectic outer world, hurry, hurry, hurry—but an illusory and comforting inner world full of outer things; warm with shaded lights. Faces in and out of the shadows so that Jack did not know if the shift of expression, the glance of eye was a trick of light or a shiver of thought.

The contrast to army life, to all previous life was so great that Jack seemed to doze on those off-duty days among the books, the music, the talk, the food, the drink—like a baby in a cot: responsible for nothing, enjoying the sensation of everything, indulged—uncritical.

71

Centred upon the unfolding self Jack had, and has, no idea of how Frank or any of the others *felt* at that time. He does not know if Frank was consciously creating round him a world to keep the harsher world outside with the snow.

If he was, Rosa and Edward made a nasty breach in the walls.

I remember the taste of the soup. I remember—but I do not. I invent them all, or re-invent them through the years. To my satisfaction, to my need for order out of chaos. To justify my journey.

There is so little on paper for reference. But it is true, I am certain, that on the day of the soup the break-up began of our life in Berlin. With that, the possibility of Frank writing *Juda Verrecka* was destroyed. To do it at all he had to do it where the crime took place. Or more fancifully, in the place where his tribe once had their territory, where the little boy was initiated into manhood, where the Mother, meaning more than mother, was betrayed and sacrificed.

Also for Jack nothing could again be the same. Frank walks away. Jolt. No more painful jokes, no more conversation, febrile overwhelming. No more size. Baby, it's cold outside.

So what led to it? History, history—with these people their past is omni-present. Jack has caught the habit.

Aunt Renata's first husband was killed trying to get out of Austria without papers. A surviving relation of that husband, an elderly woman, either a sister or a step-sister I never found out, worked in radio in East Berlin after the war.

On the Friday before the Sunday of the concert and the soup this woman gave a party to celebrate something unspecified. It was a late party, so that friends working in the theatres and the opera in East Berlin could attend after their performances.

To this party went Rosa and Edward. They borrowed Frank's Ford Popular with its GB plates.

At this time Frank's friend was a young American who wore a light tan make-up. They did not go to the party.

He was a composer. He said. Frank said that he had very great promise. He used electronic machines. He carried with him a tape of his major composition. It was called "Count Down to

Inner Space". He played it to everyone he met. He even played it to me. Sooner or later someone was going to help him to the top. In fact you only had to know Boris for ten minutes and the plug was in the socket, if you will pardon the expression.

He spoke of the composition as galactic and of the silences, there were many silences, being related to deep space. He spoke of the fear of silence in the West, the terror of cosmic silence in contrast to the ultimate achievement of silence in the East, a consummation leaving the Word behind. At that time a number of beguiling eastern gentlemen with wispy beards and the expression of chuckling babies were having a vogue. They had a system where you gave them ten per cent or more of your income and they gave you peace of mind. So it was said. It wore off later in the decade. Boris was aiming at the same market.

Frank was impressed. He said so to me in front of Boris. He said so to Rosa and Edward in front of Boris. Boris smiled his silent smile which became strained when Rosa said, "But what does he do for a living?"

He did not look right for the name Boris, but he spoke of Russian forebears and pogroms and of his grandfather who played the violin in the streets of old New York. Frank believed Boris which shows that even the sharpest mind may temporarily be blunted by passion.

Boris was not kind to Frank. Boris milked Frank.

Unfortunately the night of the party in the East zone was the night before Boris was due to fly to Hamburg with a fine-looking German boy who smiled a little like Boris smiled and said nothing at all. He seemed to have moved to the higher sphere of silence which meant so much to Boris in his, as he put it, "Structures of creativity".

Boris explained to Frank who explained to me for lack of anyone better that the German boy was *nothing* to Boris emotionally but that professionally he was of tremendous importance. Not only, by means unconnected with speech, did he inspire Boris to fresh creativity—he was influential, in some way not clearly explained, with the *Hamburgische Staatsoper*.

Even Corporal Jack doubted if they played Boris' kind of music in the Hamburg Opera House. He had been to the opera in Berlin. Twice. There was good cheap food at the interval and plenty

73

of room for exercise. It toned Jack up. He even enjoyed the singing. It bore little relation to "Count Down to Inner Space". He did not say that to Frank.

Farce that it all was, trivial and silly and ordinary (the lad on the make, the older man scruffy and voluble and generous with his shirt collar sticking up under one ear and a button off his jacket, sometimes odd socks and always ready to put his hand in his pocket) and yet—Frank suffered.

In the middle of the last poignant night there came a continuous ringing on the bell of Frank's flat.

He was barely polite when he came to the door. Rosa began at once, hysterically, to speak of their ordeal. She had lost her spectacles and her eyes seemed unnaturally large. Edward glided to the whisky and sat in a shaded corner with it. He was an expert at sinking half a bottle without being noticed. One of his skills was to make it seem natural that he should help himself from the bottle and not wait to be served by his host. The first time I met him he said quietly to me, "Pass the brown cow over would you, old chap—it needs milking". He smiled, encouraging me. There was a chip off one of his front teeth.

He was shaking like a stage character who clinks the bottle against the glass to show he is upset when Frank let him in.

Germans are either sober or rolling drunk. At the party they were soon rolling drunk. It became very loud. Things got broken. The police were called. Those East German police with the caps and the jack boots that could remind you of something. Edward took none of this seriously because he had his arm round an actress and he was not breaking anything or even singing and being sick. Suddenly it was not just the police. It was security men: documents, identity cards—and Edward is in a corner. "Who the hell is this, this foreigner spying on people who broadcast from the Democratic German Republic—why is he here?" They had seen the car. Frank's disintegrating Ford Popular with the GB plates. Clearly the vehicle of a master spy.

Rosa turned to get help from the lady who invited them, the sister or step-sister of Aunt Renata's dead husband. The faithful old comrade from the terrible thirties. Edward was waving his party card and quoting the verses that Brecht wrote in praise of Stalin (those verses suppressed from Western publications in order not to pain the consciences of the fashionable Left—as Frank put it).

A strange thing happened. All the Germans became instantly sober. All the recently friendly actors and actresses and technicians and mistresses and hangers-on became like zombies. In silence, without looking at, or speaking to, Rosa and Edward they left. They were allowed to leave. They walked away, some without their overcoats and scarves and hats and it was a freezing night.

They went by as if deaf and blind while Rosa actually clutched at arms and tried to stand in front of one or two of them. Her fine red hair came unpinned and hung about her face making her seem deranged. She still looked like it as she described her actions, believing this picture of herself to be flattering. She seriously misjudged her audience.

Boris had already appeared in the background in one of Frank's short dressing gowns. When Rosa got to the climax he yawned and said, "Oh my God!" in the accent that American professional ex-patriots seem to have in common.

She ignored him. She went on and on.

The second time he did it, ostentatiously yawning and patting his mouth, as she described their release, Edward protested from his corner with something like, "Hold on, old chap, a minute" and Frank turned on him and told him to shut up.

Rosa was immediately very rude to Boris. She was personal. She spoke of fairies. She referred obscenely to his music. It was her style. She was a woman who frequently used the word fuck. Speaking of Edward before their marriage she said, "He used to come and fuck me every Saturday night—no matter what state I was in". Quite often she told anyone unlucky enough to be nearby about her functions—or rather her malfunctions. She had a lot of things wrong with her inside. Due, Frank insisted, to the seven or eight—or was it only six?—who were knocking her off.

Boris was no match for her. The screaming began.

Even then Frank controlled himself. But Edward rose to help defend her and in passing said to Frank, "None of this would have happened if it hadn't been for your mother—they knew!"

Frank immediately picked up a chair and tried to kill him. He succeeded only in splintering a small table and breaking another

75

chair. Then he seized Edward and tried to choke him. Rosa and Boris combined to pull him off because things looked bad for Edward. Edward had never served in the armed forces because he was a Party member. He had never learned about the knee in the balls. He was definitely going to be dead in a few more minutes.

Eventually Rosa and Edward went lurching down the stairs with Frank screaming after them, "I'm sorry your friends over there didn't do to you what they did to my mother. I will if you come here again. I'll murder you both."

Just for once Boris had to do the comforting.

Aunt Renata was staying for her holiday in Rosa's flat. She was spared nothing on their return. She had the sense to leave it a day.

The next morning Frank saw Boris and his silent friend ("Isn't he *gorgeous*," Boris said softly to me when he first came to supper; he thought I'd be pleased to see the back of him. He got that right) on to a Hamburg flight at Tempelhoff. Two slender figures with identical off-white raincoats with belts that tied at the waist. Two unlined faces, lightly made up. A dark Pan-faced man in a cut-down army officer greatcoat and a fur hat smoking furiously and looking his age for once asking them to telephone the minute they got back. He paid their fares.

Another reason he never wrote a line was the allowance Jonathan made him.

He was puffy. He tended to puffiness when crossed in love. And he washed more than usual. He was very miserable that Sunday; he looked peeled as if someone had worked him over with fine emery cloth.

When Renata hesitated to speak in front of me he put a record on and sat close to one of the big speakers seeming to warm himself in the sound as if it were a fire. *The Magic Flute* and, of all people, Tauber singing.

"Edward had got a job with the BBC in television," said Renata.

"So?"

"It was arranged, settled. But the contract was not signed. Two days before he was to start they telephoned and sent for him.

When he got there the man was embarrassed. The deal was off.
No job even though all details settled, a verbal contract and so
and so!"

"Why?"

"They said they had just realized from the medical report he
had only one and a half kidneys."

Frank rocked with laughter. He was helpless. For the first time
that day, possibly that week, he enjoyed himself.

"One and a half kidneys! Oh my God—what else has he got
one and a half of? Is that why Rosa —— ? Oh how marvellous."

"Frank," said Renata patiently, "it was simply an excuse not
to employ him."

"Oh dear, oh dear, oh dear—I wonder how the half works?
One and a half —— "

"Edward went to your adopted father — "

"My *father*."

"Jack you must never speak of any of this —— "

"Don't tell him what he must not do, Renata."

"Frank I am only —— "

"Don't tell anybody what they must not do. The Nazis are
destroyed, do you understand? If you persist, you and the rest,
in these secretive absurdities you *connive*. There must be no
more connivance *ever*. Don't glare at me. I will not have any
orders given, what someone must and must not do, you understand.
Let everyone speak out and take the consequences."

—silence—

"You are right, Frank, and I am sorry."

"Sorry! Sorry—yes we all are. So Edward went to see
Jonathan and told him the BBC objected to his half kidney, and
Jonathan immediately formed a half-kidney defence society, the
HKDS for short, and held a meeting in Trafalgar Square."

"Be serious."

"Never if I can help it."

"Jonathan belongs to clubs, you know, he has powerful clients,
he is on committees and so on."

"I know! He collared the head of the Board of Governors of
the BBC and said, 'About Edward's little trouble in the waterworks —— ' "

"No! Please listen. I realize you do not wish me to tell you

77

but I must. Jonathan knows personally the man who is the head of the department where Edward was to work. They have similar views."

"Who? Edward's and the man, or Jonathan?"

"He and Jonathan. This man told Jonathan that they have a list. Edward is on it."

"A black list?"

"Yes. Because somewhere else there is a file on him. A dossier, you understand."

"Jonathan told you that?"

"He told Edward."

"That the BBC operate a black list on politically dubious people?"

"Yes."

"Which means they must have some kind of liaison with a government vetting department?"

"Yes, I did not go into that."

"So where is the evidence?"

"How can there be evidence? Don't be so stupid, Frank. There is a file. They say you are not capable of the job. Finish there."

"But we are speaking of England, Renata."

"So?"

"So—why does your son-in-law hesitate to make a case? In England you can do that, you know. Even potential traitors like Edward can do that. They make a speciality of pushing to the limit the freedom it is their firm intention to destroy, you have noticed that?"

"Do not attack me, Frank."

"You can bet your life I will, Renata—you *want* the BBC to have a black list; you *want* that unspeakable turd Edward to have a case; you *want* the Party liners to —— "

"No! I do not. It is I, not you, who see the dangers. I asked Jonathan to act. To make a case. It is not possible. The BBC are not publicly answerable and that finishes it."

"Well, my dear, as far as I am concerned I am not with Voltaire over Edward—I not only detest what he has to say (and what he stands for) I would do everything I can to prevent his saying it. In fact given a chance I'd kill the son-of-a-bitch which is what I failed to do the night before last. Trust me to miss with a chair! I think I may write a letter to the BBC pointing out that to consider employing Edward in the first place shows a lamentable lack of standards, but congratulating them on their underhand and novel method of wriggling out of the bargain. It shows real style to use a half-kidney, don't you think? I mean what do you expect in a democracy?—a society of angels? If it *is* a democracy the shits must also have their say. Mustn't they? What do you think people are? They are everything good, bad and in between—so why shouldn't parliament be two-thirds full of meat-heads, bigots, fetishists, flat earthers and market gardeners eh? Society is!"

"And Edward is out. Without right of appeal. I see!"

"Renata, I have never known you be a hypocrite, what the hell has got into you? We both know there are enough Party members, ex-Party members, fellow travellers, old Stalinists around to keep Edward in work till 1984. We could both list at least 50 in position with pull of one kind or another—enough to get that fool a job if he has any ability at all."

"So why is he here! He is working I believe!"

"I accept your apology!"

"I shall hit you, Frank!"

"Then I shall cry, dear Aunt, and you will be sorry!"

"What can you do with him, Jack?"

"Don't ask him, he's an ignorant soldier—what are you?"

His life was not a process of self discovery, it was a process of self healing. The method of monologue was to discover ideas that came only in the heat of thought and speech interacting. Sometimes people say, "I did not know I knew that, or thought that, *until I said it.*"

Momentum is everything in this. The forward rush of words— often disconnected. Sometimes to fend off something unbearable.

Perhaps Renata understood for a moment that day (only a moment, her personality was so powerfully formed it was beyond her to get inside the skin of others for any but the shortest time) that her attacks upon culture actually threatened the sanity of her nephew.

I did not realize it until I wrote it. Which places our

relationship, Frank's and mine. He had to say it to find his way. I have to write it to find mine.

Later that Sunday while Renata was still there, Frank began in a light, affectionate tone to speak cruelly of her daughter. The contrast between his attitude and his words was very strange. Could he really be saying these things in front of her mother?

"Do you know why your daughter married Edward? And he her? I will tell you—she actually believed, because she does not have a good ear, that Edward was an English gentleman: a discontented Guy Burgess sort of English gentleman. He had been to Oxford University where they handle the punt pole in a different manner from the gentlemen who go to Cambridge University; an enchanting discovery—and he had sculled about Hendon with seven other English gentlemen, and he had once shaken hands with someone who had shaken hands with John Cornford, and he spoke with feeling of the Madrid days and the International Brigade although he had never been nearer Spain than a package cruise to Majorca, paid for by someone else— she picked him up at Red Barn, a thee-ayter my dear Jack, where rough working-class reds and soft intellectual reds socked it to the faithful with what you might, to make an artistic judgement, call the destitute man's Berliner Ensemble.

"Edward could not believe his luck. 'My God,' he cried to his buddies, which was a petty bourgeois exclamation he could not kick, 'I have found Rosa, who is named after Rosa Luxembourg —she is a continental intellectual'.

"His judgement of intellectual capacity was as faulty as hers of the English class structure. 'And,' he said in his soft voice showing that chipped tooth, 'she must have rich relations. She has this cousin, Frank, who is the son of a filthy Trot (who got what she deserved because there were no sentimental flies on old Joe)—the fellow is living in the family of a rich Jew-boy doing very nicely, *and she must have other rich relations.* All my life, like a Salvation Army major surveying the sweet new girl recruits in their bonnets, I have been looking for a true believer worthy of me who is twenty years younger and will support me until the revolution (which is quite inevitable due to contradictions inherent in capitalism), when I shall take my rightful place near the head of society—even if it is classless. To be practical, you fellows, all

Jewish, continental, intellectual girls like her *do have* rich relations even if Mum, in this case, is a little potty (due to some nasty business in the late thirties which we don't speak of because none of us ever mentions a certain pact that Joe was forced to sign with Adolf because of the chicanery of the capitalist class) and insists on sweating over a hot stove in what is barely a workers' caff somewhere in darkest Balham! No, no, you chaps—that caff is a front—and we all know about *them*! In fact how could she, my beloved, or dozens like her, have got here at all unless the family was able to raise enough gold bars and give half of them to the SS? (who always made a profit you will remember). And I think you'll agree that even though Jewish families think daughters are not actually human beings like sons they do get their share. And my view of marriage is that what is hers is mine.'

"(Between us, Jack, he was getting his share already. In those Red Barn days when the Free German Youth and the Young Communist League and similar *apparatchiks* were not busy fornicating they used to copulate—the fellows were utterly dedicated to giving, and the girls to receiving, the jolly thing; and as one once remarked to me, 'If it all stops tomorrow I've had my share'. It forced the rabbits of Great Britain to issue a press statement saying that compared to these eager believers in a Socialist future and round the clock jig-a-jig they considered themselves celibate and could odious comparisons please cease.)

"Deep in his cups, that is to say someone else's whisky, his voice trembling a little like a man who knows he has won the pools but not yet actually held the cheque in his hands, Edward would murmur to himself, 'I shall never have to work again!' We all had delusions in those days—including Rosa, of course. She gazed mistily past Edward's frayed cuffs and Party card at the Anthony Eden moustache and the crinkles round his eyes from hiding his real expression and said, 'How wonderful! He is not only a lifetime believer, he is twenty years older and he alone recognizes my true worth. He lets me talk all the time—*and he will give me security.*'

"Security, Jack! That is what all us displaced objects lust after. A little safe home in the West. Renata has done it all on her own. My dear! how she sweats to pay off that mortgage on the little terraced haven. And look at me! Jonathan would never have given his own son an allowance past the age of 21! Never! But for me? A minimum 1,500 a year from here to eternity. He knows, does Jonathan. So can you blame little Rosa my cousin?

"But there is a problem. The past and the Party never let go. Consider today's events. Press the button and I nearly walk out under the traffic. (Oh mother dear, what is this 'ere, that looks like strawberry jam?) And look at the pair of them, two nights ago, crossing to the east full of hope and hypocrisy—I mean what is more natural—longing for it to feel right, to feel like home— *I've got it!*"

Aunt Renata turned her back on him.

"I—have—got—it," he said again, "and you *knew*."

Aunt Renata did not turn round.

"They went for a job, didn't they? The show-biz party was either a screen or a lie, wasn't it?"

"Yes," said Renata, "it was."

"And that's why you're frightened on my behalf?"

"Yes."

"Because they went to be vetted and somehow they screwed it. The comrades, the true believers just like them, instantly betrayed them. It was to be a propaganda job in East German radio, was it?"

"That was not specified."

"The reason they got back here is they are not worth the publicity, or their keep in one of Ulbrecht's prisons; there is no mileage in them because they are nonentities. They came to me to cuddle up. They had been scared witless. *And rejected.* Fancy that! Neither the BBC nor East German radio—nobody loves them. Including me."

"You are the trouble," said Renata.

"Oh how stupid of me! Of course I am. They are related to the son of a heretic; and he is living in the West zone and he consorts with soldiers and Americans—and of course the Americans must be CIA (can't you see Boris in the CIA, Jack? and you must be army intelligence!) What cretins they all are."

"No worse I suppose," said Jack, "than our blokes sending someone to feel my collar because I know you and you know Edward—if Aunt Renata has got it right."

82

"I have," she said, "coffee?"

While she made it she said, "I knew Ulbrecht. He got out after the Reichstag Fire. He hated her even then."

"Who?"

"My mother," said Frank, "you would expect that."

"I know I'm thick," said Jack, "but I don't see, not really, why they got the boot the other night."

"OK. Take as a starting point the Nazi-Soviet pact of 1939. The Russians did a deal with the Nazis not only on the military side but on the political. If Himmler would release some of the good comrades and true from his concentration camps, then Stalin would turn over those poor, silly, deluded bastards, Jew and non-Jew, who had taken refuge in the Soviet Union believing themselves safe from the Gestapo and the SS. This disgusting exchange took place. The torture and murders followed.

"In the case of my mother, who had been caught early in 1939, and was in a camp of course, the comrades could have got her out. Instead they not only left her, they agreed to her murder along with a lot of others who were deviationist in some way. Heretics must die. Had she got out by herself the comrades would have killed her if they could. It was the purges and —— that is a digression.

"To come to two nights ago. My mother was well known. There was naturally a file on her in Moscow and on her relations, her friends. This would have been regularly updated through the years. So what happened was this—the East Germans, as a matter of routine, got the dossiers from the KGB in Moscow, no I really am not joking, their archives are formidable. When that eager pair with their carefully packed bags turned up (incidentally, Renata, I'd never have seen my car again, would I? It was no off-the-cuff decision, they must have been arranging it for weeks! My God they are cheeky!) Anyway, when they turned up and said, 'Here we are, when do we start work?' (I've just *realized*— the show-biz party was for *them*. Your first husband's sister or whatever she is was their sponsor wasn't she, Renata? That's it— I'll bet she's sorry! If she's lucky she's only been demoted to scrubbing floors)—the reception committee said, 'There's a nasty ideological skeleton clacking about in your cupboard; you are not pure; there is a smell on the landing, who's paying you to spy over here? The CIA? M16?' They are hard-line Stalinist in East Germany and will be until someone chops Ulbrecht if they ever do. Do you see, Jack?

"Even if cuddly old mass murderer Nikki Krushchev is ascendent in Mother Russia at the moment and saying very sharp things about the late Uncle Joe *nothing has basically changed*. Paranoid and murderous suspicion reign supreme.

"And what do you expect? Ask yourself how many centuries the Inquisition was in business looking after God's party line. If you don't know ask me!

"I'll sum it up. It's hard for a simple, Anglo-Saxon lad like you to believe but, like doing sums at school, you've got to accept that in the same way that two and two make four my mother, who was murdered in early 1940 (the Nazis doing the Stalinists a favour), was responsible for the niece that she never saw and the niece's husband (who holds the same beliefs as those who had her murdered) getting a going-over by East German security people and then being booted out and told not to come back. I suspect that it was Edward's credentials and the fact they both held British passports that saved them from a very much nastier time spread over a few months.

"The past and the Party never let go—let's drink to that."

Late that night. Renata leaving. Renata uneasy, something has still not been said. Frank drinking, steadily drinking. There seem less lights on than usual. Jack has been sitting in the darkest corner writing in his WD exercise book.

Frank said, "We have changed rôles, it seems."

"No."

"But I understand now why you are so conveniently here, on holiday at this time; Renata you have aided and abetted."

"She is my daughter."

"To wrap up the flat. To take home the stuff not wanted. To make the prepared statement if anyone is vaguely interested."

"I love her. I thought they might find some happiness."

"You—thought—what?"

"For them, Frank, a more congenial atmosphere."

"I like that. The congenial atmosphere of East Berlin. Would it do as a holiday slogan do you think—come and enjoy the congenial——."

"I hate them over there as much as you. But she is my daughter."

"Ah! Then at least you will understand something, Renata— it hurts you cruelly that I speak of her as I do, I know, I know; and I will never mention any of it again. But please, I beg you say no more to me *ever* about the things that I," his arm slopping drink from the glass indicates books, music, "cherish."

"I promise you."

"Drink to it?"

"I must go."

"One drink. Jack? Have you a glass? Renata, here take this one, for you, vodka, for me whisky, for Jack—Jack?"

"I am just writing something down, Frank, while I think of it."

"Ah, you see Renata he is my faithful pupil, my disciple—or is that a report for the authorities when you return?"

"Course it is, Franky."

"And he dissembles well. He is very, very quick. Sometimes he does not think I notice. I shall miss him."

Jack felt a sense of shock.

"You going somewhere, Frank?"

"Oh yes. Can't stay here much longer, kid. Now then, whisky for you?"

"Yes."

"I drink to love and art and the death of tyrants."

Before I put him to bed.

"You never asked how I knew about Red Barn and all that; you wanted to—I watched you. Can't you guess? I was *in* the Free German Youth, I was *in* the Young Communist League. Of course I was. Just like the Ha-Jot, old cock. Anything but anything, if I could have the company. Be one of them not one of me. But I could not, I fear, I went through the motions but was separated by vast spaces, by ranges of ice mountains, by hollow places in myself because I was not them."

When he lay in bed, eyes shut, both hands clasped round his genitals.

"18b was the order to intern and there I was my poor father

already so ill they had him in the infirmary and round me men and boys secretive and violent and someone came to me and said are you Frank and I said I am I am and they said the word has come through Lisbon and I said where is that and they said speak softly don't show your feelings the word has come through Lisbon your mother is dead and you know why and I said no I don't know why and they told me what she was my mother I heard it for the first time and I said what does it mean a Trotskyite and someone turned from a wall leaned from a bunk seemed to fall almost on me and said oh there's a clever boy just like his mother what does it mean hey hey hey hey hey hey and then a little man was there fierce as a hawk taking me by the hand saying come along Frank I am Jonathan and in his house it was warm and safe but from habit I stood by the door when he went out until he came back and would not move although I did not wet myself but dreamed all night that he would die and I would be sent away and his wife was unhappy and when he came back on the third or the fourth day I said can I stay with you forever Jonathan I said it in German and he replied in German and said of course you can stay as long as you like and after two years I believed he was telling the truth and my real father went to a skeleton and died and I was not there on his last day but Jonathan was there and after that I became Jonathan's son and I wish he was here today this day because I am not sane I am not quite sane and when Jonathan is there it is safe don't put out the light please don't put out the light don't leave me."

What did it mean? Deviationist? Heretics?

We stopped the Land Rover just past the tar ramp. We cleared it spreading to the walls. Voices soft soft, taps on the shoulder fingers pointing watch your backs, it's over there but looking up and round first for the ambush, for the snipers. No shots.

The light was growing but it was still darker than twilight and freezing. The bundle in the road was making sounds. Bad sounds. You cannot always tell if they are dying by the sounds. Perhaps he was booby trapped.

We picked him up and got him away. A lot of things had been done to him. We knew him. A taxi driver. A Protestant. He wanted to die. He kept saying so. He died. He had been rompered. They had him all night in a Romper Room.

Romper Room was the title of an American television programme for the kiddie winkies shown on Ulster TV. Often pretty ladies read pretty stories to all the pretty teenies.

The Prods called their torture chambers Romper Rooms. They used lock-up garages and other places that were easy to hose down. Sometimes the voices of the victims were heard crying for mercy or release. In vain.

The taxi driver was a Prod, the torturers were Prods. The taxi driver had deviated. He was a sly, sometimes pissed-up, can I shake you by the hand, sorr, to show no hard feelings you're a gentleman, sort of feller.

Also a heretic. His punishment was not simply death. It was torture until he begged for death. What they had done to him made you shiver.

We rented colour TV sets inside our fortress. The lads tuned three of them to *Romper Room*. They stripped naked in front of the pretty lady. They daubed each other head to toe with camouflage paint green and black—head to toe. They crawled on all fours, they shouted and pranced and waved their choppers at her, they wiped finger stains of paint on the walls like infants dabbling in their own excreta.

I kept the pistol they had left in his jacket. Or planted? He killed someone he shouldn't have, I suppose. Who cared?

The lads shouted obscene things at the pretty lady. They got him out of their mind's eye.

Now I had *seen* what happened to Frank's mother. If it happened to that taxi driver it could happen to anyone. Perhaps it happened to Frank.

IV

JACK STANDS IN the hotel window recess. He folds back the wooden shutters in their three leaves. One floor below the hotel sign creaks upon its horizontal support, not to the wind but to the passing of container lorries every half hour that seem to scrape the building.

To his right through glass blooming with sea mist from early morning the softened outline of walls, fences, gutted houses declining into the earth. Ruins soon, like a Roman town a Greek city upon a promontory ready for tourists. To his left the ancient shipyard, empty and silent behind its high wall. A huge ship's propeller, baulks of timber, grass between a set of narrow-gauge lines.

The container lorry seems to grind its gearbox to pieces as it turns the corner, scrapes between hotel and shipyard wall; the trapped sound batters at the brickwork either side and the whole room trembles under Jack's naked feet.

Above the lorry the sign groans. On it the painted flag strains eternally against the painted halyard. It is the red flag they flew at the main in wooden ship days when the guns were run out and the sailors, naked to the waist, fierce as wolves, looked at the enemy and said "For what we are about to receive ..." and then put match to touch hole for the first broadside. The Battle Flag.

Jack is writing at a rickety table. He hesitates to name the town. It is still like a dream that needs interpreting. Lotus land of alleys under driven clouds. Grey northern light. No steel disc of sun. It is not real.

The yellow bulldozer is real which clears the site of a burned weatherboard house. It crunches backward over head-high weeds through a hole smashed in railings. It swivels to empty the black filth, the rags, the charred furniture ends and the run of ooze like tar into the council lorry. One wall of the place still stands like a façade on a film set. It has burned-out windows and through them the sky both ways.

The container lorry edges past the council lorry, after that it's clear all the way to the new dock in the town five miles up the road. The continental ferry will soon go there as well, but for the moment it still uses the old pier opposite as it has for a century, to the very front door of The Battle Flag Hotel—three-storey, rambling, almost empty, AA 2 star—place of revelation for Jack and Gwen.

Jack writes the word Battletown and decides to call it that. Gwen enters the room behind him and closes the door softly. Her hair is wet from the bath. She is naked under her dress. She is barefoot. She is also shivering with cold. She puts on Jack's coat.

"What are you writing?"

"That it has taken over two months for the bulldozer to come to the burned house."

"They are sort of starving them out."

"What?"

"The council in the new town."

"Who?"

"The survivors here. The old ones that come to the shop. The council doesn't mend the roads any more, or replace broken street lamps for ages. They only do the dustbins every other week."

"Oh?"

"They want to flatten it all and put up something else."

"Housing estate?"

"Oh no. Factories. I don't think you're interested."

"It would make a good army training ground as it stands."

"What for?"

"Street fighting, sniping—urban guerrilla warfare, from here, looking down like this you command——"

"There are a lot of rats and the cellars fill with water."

—silence—

"He must have come for some very *strong* reason."

"Your friend."

"Yes. He could never stick his own company for 30 seconds usually. And in this place!"

"Oh he wasn't on his own."

"No?"

89

"The others were German."

—silence—

"What's the matter, Jack?"

"How many Germans?"

"I saw two."

"Saw?"

"I came in here."

"*Here?*"

"The bar downstairs, it's the best place to be taken for a drink at lunchtime. He was with two of them, I remember, because——"

"Because you notice things! I mean you could hardly miss two Germans in this place. No one could."

"A butch girl and a skinny fellow with a beard like D. H. Lawrence."

"But there was nothing about that at the inquest. And when I spoke to Beatrice the day before yesterday she——"

—silence—

"Are you angry with me?"

"No. No."

"You're miles away and you look——"

"I don't understand how they could have missed it—here in this empty place—when I came in your shop yesterday I caused enough stir—that old boy coming up, asking if I was going to start a firm, bring some life back."

"But you're a stranger."

"And the Germans are *not*?"

"Oh no! We're used to them. We get a lot of them through and other foreigners. On the ferry. I mean not dozens, but enough; ever since the yard closed. The Germans have an optical instrument place up the road, a big factory, didn't you see it when you drove here?"

"No. It was dark."

"That's why the council want to flatten all this. Just leave the hotel, then with this and the yard they can put up plenty of factories. The Canadians are going to——"

"Were they his friends?"

"I don't know. They might just have been over for a meeting.

The German directors come once or twice a year and the local managing director is a German himself."

"A butch girl and D. H. Lawrence don't sound like members of anybody's board."

"I don't know. If he was lonely he'd talk to anyone, wouldn't he? It's natural in a bar."

"Yes he would. Oh yes he would."

"The local managing director has a Mercedes and a chauffeur. I went to school with the chauffeur. He's very randy, have you noticed how randy chauffeurs are?—do you think it's the job makes them randy or randy fellers look for the job?"

"Hmm."

"And have you noticed how men make love the way they drive?"

"Hmm."

"And have you noticed I'm frightened?"

"Why?"

"Because I'm here with you and now everybody knows; and last night I didn't care but it's now the morning after and I can't get near you. Because I'm afraid you're not loving, you have a terrible expression which frightens me."

"I am loving."

"Not really loving, the way you put it so poetically—because no one had ever talked to me like that, last night—but if you're not then tell me."

"I am a loving man."

"I've been left before but I want to know."

Jack lifts her up and holds her, embraces her touching the softness of her breasts and the inside of her arms, under his coat over her shoulders through her dress. Jack smells her putting his nose close to the downy part of her neck under the hair near the nape. She puts her arms round him, holds his head with one hand. They close their eyes and begin to rock to and fro with their bodies close but not fiercely held together.

"You will have to reassure me every day."

"I will."

"You are hard again I feel you."

"Of course I am."

"It's so flattering."

"Lie down."

"No, no."

"Why not?"

"Will they come with the breakfast? I'm frightened they will."

"Not yet. Lie down. Look I'll tidy the bed, make it unsordid, spread it, it's still warm. Look at the sheet that was under us!"

"Are you sure? Are you sure?"

"Don't you want to? To welcome the day."

"Touch me and you will see."

"That is beautiful. That is like honey, like nectar, like the juice of pomegranates. You look wanton with your skirt up like that."

"Please check the lock."

"I'll shove the chair back under the handle."

"I've never been able to look at someone in the light like this, to talk my true feelings, some crude, some ordinary, some . . ."

Jack's clothes upon the floor. Sheet and blankets over them to keep out the cold. The seed still running out of her from the night. Quiet time.

"Are you sore?"

"No. I was afraid you might be. Jack?"

"No. There, there does it touch in the right place."

"Oh God yes. And I want you to tongue me. That is beautiful, like that, like that; the way you did in the night. Nobody ever. Oh I do like that. And let me, let me."

Where has all past energy, ambition, courage, brutality and high endeavour gone? Down the graveyard every one in Battletown, save thee and me, lady, whom I cover; in whom I move slow and tired for it is morning and all night we lay together, exploring. It is possible I will not come, not spill my seed, not shoot like the broadsides of the night and I shall not care because with thee my heart's blood nothing is failure everything is sharing. One tiny corner of my mind, detached, considers Germans, wonders if they were passing acquaintances struck up and dropped like matches in a pub lunch hour. Or Germans of another sort?

Beatrice was *indifferent*. That is what the separate functioning corner of the brain cannot understand, cannot assimilate, cannot *accept*. Your eyes are closed, the lids flicker and you stare at me a second but you are looking inwards and your thighs and the globes of your soft arse in my hands move in a rhythm that chimes with mine and does not force us to the edge too early. And Frank and Beatrice felt like this, he never lied that day in Charlotte Street, how would I feel if this woman were to die choked with smoke, part burned, cooked meat on the bone?

"What's the matter, what's the matter?"

"Nothing, my darling, because you are alive, safe, here with me."

Now all my mind is with you. Your lips are a little parted and I listen with joy to the sounds you make, the words you speak and then I am no longer anywhere but in my loins all senses are there and your hand is across my mouth to muffle me shouting in exaltation.

The rapping on the door.

"Leave it outside."

Clink clink on the floor. Whispering and laughing in the bed.

"Timing what timing!"

"Hungry; aren't you?"

"I've never been so hungry."

"I must wash."

"So must I."

"You've just had a bath."

"Come on, share the basin with me."

"The towels are soaking!"

"It was my bath, sorry!"

"Never mind, never mind."

"Let me wash you, let me, let me. Like this, that's nice."

"Then I will you."

"This is very French, isn't it, wish there was a bidet, why don't I feel guilty?"

"Why don't I?"

"There is something I haven't told you."

"There's plenty of time."

"I have a child, Jack."

"So do I."

"I thought so, I thought so. You will leave me."

"No Bea, I won't."

"Why do you say Bea—is that you wife, Bea? Is that it?"

"No I said it deliberately because Frank's sister is Bea and Bea both loved and tormented Frank."

"Oh?"

"And when he told me I didn't really understand."

"You do now?"

"I begin to."

"Don't lie to me, will you? Try not to lie to me even if it's difficult to say."

"I'll try."

"How it changes every few minutes. I was out of my mind with happiness just now and before that so miserable I nearly ran away, and now——"

"And now it's breakfast."

"Anyone out there?"

"No. We have the museum to ourselves."

"When I said I have a child."

"You were saying you could not leave it."

"Yes."

"Everything changes. In six months you may not want to."

"In six months you will be fed up with me if I torment you already!"

"I'll tell you then."

"If you do I'll kill you."

"That's reasonable, my lovely!"

Jack and Gwen eat sausages, eggs, bacon; they drink all the tea, eat all the toast, the smears of butter in greasy foil, scrape out four small plastic pots of marmalade, pause, and then finish the milk in the jug between them.

In the mirror their faces have not changed since yesterday which surprises them. They say to each other, as they regard their images, you don't look like that and nor do you, and on the way out (there is a back way straight into the alleys) she speaks self consciously and too loud of making jewellery and the kind of safe in which the gold and silver is kept at night and how all the grains of it are carefully preserved when working—such valuable crumbs must not fall to glitter in cracks in the work-room floor.

The morning air and a transistor somewhere in the soft mist peep-peep-peep-peep-peeyupping the hour on the BBC and the inevitable bad news. Outside the shop the first old head, in head scarf, neckless above its plump, swathed body and thick ankles

94

sprouting from carpet slippers: immediately Gwen is raucous and laughing and the screech of English mums and grandmums, another has arrived in curlers, dyed black hair, eyes like a blackbird, false teeth white as an enamel wash basin, water running; laughter, weather, family, gotter letter, dear; all eyes not looking at, most carefully looking at Jack the soldier who stands like a spare flute at a wedding and before he knows is inside and helping carry things, light the standup oil fire.

They all guess what's going on; signal their approval, with sly looks redfaced laughter, that Gwen being a fine woman in her prime (some of them have met her husband, don't think much of him, Jack learns afterwards on the shingle beach) should have a little on the side and good luck to her. She'll be like them soon enough, all the men down the graveyard except nowadays its 30 miles away and it's the crematorium.

The first wave recedes. Gwen speaks in her other voice, quietly; uneasy in this new public situation, expecting him to find an excuse to leave. Is he surprised they speak without modesty (a cucumber in her hand—watch where you put that, Gwen!—hey hey hey hey hey—and she replied it's got a bend in it—hey hey hey hey hey) about families gone away, won't write, seldom return; gruesome illnesses in internal detail? Nothing private here, all in the same boat: when they were young it was a fine, well-manned cross-Atlantic steamer—today an old hull stuck in the mud, up the creek. Soon to be a ribbed skeleton. No he is not surprised. He feels at home.

"Cup o' tea?"

"Why not!"

"I'll make it."

"Who else?"

Jack has caught the tone.

Musical the sound of the bell on the twist of metal. Round the door in slow time a pensioner's head, tremendous nutcracker in profile, engraved by Durer, national-health spectacles upon the nose. The head speaks cheerfully of solitude and cold. Gwen places small amounts of food in the oil-cloth shopping bag far too large. Takes the money. Agrees that she, too, will never be happy with the little decimal coins a penny in the old days was big and solid. Yes but that's all gone. How is her auntie? Still up the hospital that is too bad but the old head is very cheered because he is not there yet and her auntie is younger, where did she have the growth? oh *veins* that is very nasty but it's ever so good of Gwen to keep her little business going.

He lingers by the oil stove passes large hands over it back and forwards through the rising warmth. The nutcracker opens wide to show the last stubborn teeth and he is smiling at his thoughts, I'll tell you a joke before I go, you always do, Mr Thirkettle— and he does hey hey hey hey hey until the bell rings over, and the door closes on, the laughter; and the woman turns to the soldier.

"And he means before he *goes*! Will he survive to the end of the alley? Cheer up, soldier, I love uniforms where's yours?"

"I left it behind."

"Never mind, chief, it's not the cloth it's the man inside, en it?"

"That's it."

"You gotter photo? I'd like somethin' to remember you by."

"I'll send you one."

—silence—

"Is it dangerous in Ireland?"

"Depends where you are."

"For you."

"No."

"I can tell when you're lying."

"Oh?"

"You look at me too honestly!"

"I'll have to watch that."

"You don't really trust me, do you?"

"What do you mean?"

"I can never shut up, that's the trouble—I'm sort of direct action."

"I know!"

"I could hit you but I won't because I don't want to be hit back, would you do that?—it's all sex you realize and I'm playing hard to get."

A moment ago sympathizing with the smallness of pensions, shortness of breath (that's what we all die of in the end, shortness of breath, hey hey hey hey hey) twists in old backs that have borne too much weight. She loves them all right. Loves her own

96

people. But never gives them an ounce over weight and counts the money carefully. Saving auntie's inheritance for as long as she can.

Facing me now, quite a different woman. In one way she is like a cat. She is incapable of an ugly movement. A continuous pleasure to look at. And I do not trust her any more than I trust anyone on earth over some things. Like Frank in Battletown.

She catches the thought. As I used to with Frank, and I'm unprepared.

"Your friend? He's got the edge on me this morning, I can feel it."

Make a joke of it.

"Do you think I'm queer, really?"

"Course you are! Same as I'm keen on my brother."

"Are you?"

"It's natural; and you're not, just your feminine side works better than most men, it doesn't seem to trouble you. And you're complicated."

"Like you. And very sexy."

"You make me."

"You encourage me, let's go in the back of the shop."

"No! No! No!—that's auntie's, we couldn't in there or I'd have brought you back last night."

"Oh yes!"

"Don't laugh at me or I will hit you, I'd like to, it would do us both good except——"

"You don't want me to, just wrestle like this."

"Not *here*."

—silence—

"Why did you get married, Jack?"

"Rebound."

"Oh?"

"The second one like you wouldn't marry me."

"She was a fool."

"She was afraid."

"That you would betray her?"

"No!"

"Sorry."

"That I would be killed."

"I'm afraid of that, now."

In Charlotte Street Frank, speaking of Beatrice, said, "But we adore each other. We are besotted. We wear each other out, not with love-making but with our feelings, our caring for each other, our fears for each other. It is incomprehensible and we each distrust it looking behind the eyes for treachery."

As Jack and Gwen look at each other for a moment, it passes.

"It can happen anytime, dying—I saw the place where my parents' car went over the cliff. He was no fool, my old man, old Chasser—a mug, yes—sometimes a bit easily persuaded but not stupid. The edge of the cliff was unfenced with a nice run of grass verge lifting a little into the sky giving a kind of false perspective. Children sometimes took a run at it they told me locally. Following a ball, you know?

"And they won't fence it?"

"No. Nor is there any local demand."

"But that is not what you're talking about anyway."

"No."

"Something to do with Frank?"

"Yes. Incongruity."

"And to do with me?"

"Yes. Now I know how he felt about Beatrice. And how she must have felt about him. And yet she was *indifferent* when I talked to her. She faked her feelings. And there was something else. Fear, I think. You know the way you can smell it?"

"No."

"You can when you . . ."

"What?"

"Nothing."

"Let's go for a walk, I'll put up the 'back in half an hour' sign."

We walk, wrapped to the neck against the cold, the bitter damp air making our faces red.

If I have a friend, and that friend dies because he is so full of dope he doesn't smell the smoke, I might consider looking for the pusher, because there has to be a pusher, and dealing with him. But if my friend has an adopted sister and an adopted father who both know, for certain, that my friend does not ever take drugs, then I might think the first idea simple-minded. I am sure about my friend and the drugs because he tried them all in turn

98

as a deliberate experiment before the drug situation was commonplace, and boasted of the fact he was, in quotes, immune. It is like being a gambler. Either you are or you're not. And in any case his release was booze although again he was not alcoholic.

If I know, or think I know, that my friend is most passionately involved with his sister, in quotes, and she reciprocates; and if I know that his father is slightly unhinged in the direction of civil rights and is by profession a solicitor—how is it that nothing was said at the inquest by either of them?

Further if I know that many of the people with whom he and his family are, or were, involved are actively political and his mother was murdered, as a Trotskyite, by the connivance of the Communists with the Nazis after the Soviet-Nazi pact of 1939, and that things happened in Berlin to Rosa and Edward only fourteen or so years ago as a direct result of that; and if . . .

I did not say a word of it to her as we walked a moment ago. I listened to her childhood and looked at empty spaces that she filled with pubs and cookshops and sweetshops; I heard in the muffling air the tramp of the sailors filling the street as they marched to the marine band, while the tradesmen looked out of their empty eye sockets through the long smashed glass upon the last of England. Their starched aprons are their shrouds.

No wonder Jack and Gwen clench tight their arms together and stop by a barrier of railway sleepers set vertical, a wall smelling of tar, and kiss stroking with their tongues sensing the shortness of their day.

PART THREE

V

I WENT INTO a teashop with him once. Old ladies and brass warming pans and not somewhere you would expect to find them, not Bath or Cheltenham but, of all places, Chatham on the London road. I remember that someone officious told him to do something—to wait, or to stand to one side, or to hang up his hat, or to come back in ten minutes: one of those helpful people who love public order and keep you outside in the queue when the cinema is half empty.

Frank stood clenching his fists. Then he began to shout but he could not get the words out because he stammered. I had never heard him like it in public. He was so enraged he spat as he spoke, the saliva flying, "Don't g-g-g-give m-m-m-m-m-me orders d-d-d-d-do y-y-y-y-y-y-y-you hear, not in this c-c-c-c-c-country, —not here—*not in this country.*"

It was a scene, all right. It took hours to pass.

He was like it again on the burning June day three years ago when he had hay fever and his face seemed folded into dozens of creases and he looked out at me from a kind of darkness. Red in the face he was, puffy eyes and guzzling the wine, cutting it with spa water to save the liver, gobbling the Italian food and the sauce marking the front of his shirt.

I, too, was like it. Just back from the first tour in Ulster. Dead friends and not free to fire until fired on.

At first when he talked about Beatrice he tried to make it light. How had it happened? He was 50 that year and it had been going on since he was 46 and she something over 30. And yet they had known each other all their lives. Brother and sister!

She had always adored him, elder brother, wise brother who deliberately played the hero, sought the uncritical admiration the warmth of it. There was no danger in it, how could there be? All in the family. We knew a thing or two about that in our village. Mostly it was dads and daughters. I did not say it. The other reason I was ill tempered, censorious and unsympathetic was I knew *for sure*, something he did not know about Beatrice. I wondered if he was having me on. Saying one thing and meaning another? Looking for support?

So I was sharp and cheerful and said, "It may feel like incest but it isn't so what's the fuss about?"

I very nearly went the whole disgusting pig and asked him what it was like to have a woman after all those willowy lads he used to fancy. I am ashamed of that. It is quite simple. He had a new pupil. She was inspired by him. Or so I thought until I met her. I was jealous. (The things I learn from my heart's desire! When Gwen looks at me with hatred because I speak, incautiously, of my child or of a journey I must make without her! Then Jack the biter is bit, feels the sharp, uneven teeth of jealousy but comes back for more—why? A mystery. We are bound together. So were Frank and Beatrice. His pupil, therefore, in all things. But I did not know three years ago what I do now.)

"It was guilt, I think," he said, "it's the power of the thing I'm talking about. She used to shout in the middle of the night 'You are taking my soul, absorbing me—please don't, please don't'. Now Jack—am I not a rational man?"

I laughed and said, "Anything but that."

It stung him and he replied sharply, "I mean, you literal fellow, unpredictable I may be but I have no more truck with souls than with flying saucers."

"That's true."

"It terrified me. It terrified us both. She would say, 'I adore you but go away from me, brother—please go'. Of course I went. When I got back to my flat the 'phone was ringing, 'Please don't leave.' I would say, 'I don't want to, I don't want to'. And I meant it. Me! The relief I felt all the way home, to be free of it, to lead my own life again changed in the second I heard her voice. I rush back. This happened a dozen times in the last four years. We engorge each other. That seems all that matters. There are no limits. Guilt is a terrible and necessary sauce to the meal.

"The first year it was wonderful. Not a cloud in the sky! Illusions! illusions, my boy! Frank might have a son, even. Eh? Be a Jewish patriarch? Hear a small voice say '*Abba*'. Settle in Swiss Cottage and light the seven-branched candles. Bar Mitzvah for the boy at the Dorchester, eh? How is that for fantasy? Start a new line like the Pharaohs of Egypt from brother and (almost) sister. My God! our descendants might have taken over Marks and Spencers even—what do you say?

"But next stop the wailing wall and I did not have to go to Jerusalem. Because why?—I will tell you why. I see from your face you wish I would speak more softly—I will not because I have hay fever and I am getting drunk and my heart aches and I am going to be a total and un-British disgrace. More wine, *compadre,* more of this bad wine you serve and make 200 per cent profit, a whole carafe, *si si* and more San Pellegrino and I am pleased that you are happy, you should be so lucky, old sport. Where was I?"

"The wailing wall!"

"After the hallucinating first year—then began the talk of souls in the night—and worse. Such Jewish, I nearly said Levantine, antics made me shiver with fear—become actually cold with goose pimples and a strong desire for hot sweet tea. Like the day I came back from France, the record business you remember—a little piracy? She was enraged I went without her, but she would not go with me because of her business, that spurious business of hers! So of course I 'phoned. Have you ever telephoned from France, from a small town? Have you queued? Have you been told every half hour that it will be only fifteen minutes and then finally have you endured half the French nation listening because you have to bellow? Have you ever shouted 'I love you, my darling Bea' at the top of your voice in an open box in a French post office?—I hope you have not—nor heard the voice at the other end flat, lifeless, dead, dead, dead to torment you because you are so far away —no response, no affection, catatonic misery, neurosis—what the hell!

"I rush back, taxi from Heathrow to her flat. I have my key, she knows I'm coming, I go in, calling, no sound, I know she is there. But is she there dead? Is it the overdose? I go through the place. And I find her!"

He drank. He glowered at the people at the next table who hardly dared clink a fork on a plate not to miss a word—it is not often you get all this and a meal as well.

"I found her in the bedroom against a wall in the corner. A shape. I put the light on. There is a way a small animal crouches on a vet's table waiting for the hypodermic. She said nothing, did not move; she was crying. I went to her and she—not exactly screamed because it was not above a whisper, but it seemed like a scream—I must not touch her or I, too, would be infected by—whatever it was had hold of her. She said, 'I am in danger, I am in deadly danger, can't you see?'

"All right I will speak softly because now it is serious. She was ill. With what? From what? The guilt? I had it too. I was helpless. How useless it feels? I have seen you do it to me, don't look surprised you will recognise it—to stand beside someone in distress —but what does it mean, distress? Their flesh is intact, the belly comfortably full of food, all the pipes working, heart lungs liver and lights all humming away; and they tell you that inside something torments them, something that if you could see it on the flesh would be as terrible as third-degree burns. You can't see it, you can't measure it, you can't anoint or bandage it. You can drug it, of course, or do what she was doing and I did not know for a time. She went to a quack, you know the one, what's his name— Medlock. Not a shrink—a faith and spirit healer would you believe! He knew rich and impressionable material when he saw it. He knew how to whip up the hysteria, make them terrified and dependent. A proper little black-hearted Svengali, that gentleman.

"He got out on top of the boom and is nicely settled near Cannes now. The women still trek down there to have the hands laid on if you'll pardon the expression. His partner was an Indian gentleman with a dubious medical degree and they ran an abortion clinic on the side. Pay ready cash. Ladies flew in from all over for one sort of cure or the other. I know because I had him investigated."

"You did!" I was astonished. Usually if there was trouble you looked round for Frank and found a warm space.

"Yes I did," he said.

He stammered as he said it. When he saw me look at his clenched hands on the table he put them underneath.

"I could have killed him," he said and I took him seriously. I remembered Edward.

"I wanted a chum of mine to do an exposé in a colour supp. I took him the material. He never did it."

The area round his plate was like a painter's palette. He took some pills and then squirted with a small atomiser up his nose. He carried an entire packet of paper handkerchiefs and the sodden balls were piling up in the ashtray. I thought of asking for another table. But he had been here before, and overtipped before. The small Italian waiter, a trainee, set about it. When it was clear I said, "So what happened?"

"It was up to me," he said.

"You mean you got treatment for her?"

"No," he said. "Don't you see—*it had to be me*. I had to get her through it because I caused it. I adored her. She wasn't always in that state—but it was terrifying when she was. I understood only one thing. That I had to love her without counting the cost. Now here's a turn-up, warrant officer, for one as unstable as myself. But that, perhaps, is why I could do it. Besides she is Jonathan's daughter. Can you think of a greater betrayal? To abandon Jonathan's daughter?"

I did not like Jonathan's daughter the only time I met her. I found it hard to picture her in what he was saying. I now realize he would have found Gwen equally improbable.

He sat with Beatrice for hours either in silence or to reason with her. Reason instead of passion! She demanded the truth. The price of her remaining sane, the price of her trust in him was that he must not lie in the smallest particular.

This was not said directly. For long periods their relationship was normal or ecstatic or just dull. They joked about her outbursts at these times. But when the darkness came down there was an unspoken contract imposed from outside them, from God knows where, and recognized by them both. Truth for sanity. She could immediately detect lies, evasions, dishonest silences.

It was a battle. He had to tell her things she loathed to hear; things that no man in his senses would tell his woman; in return he had to bear her hatred, her violence for the suffering she made him cause her. Often he was afraid of her.

He had to resist the normal impulse to cut and run; or to react in anger and rend her in turn—or worst of all, to cut her off from his heart to save his feelings. She tested him to destruction for two years. He bore it because he loved her. He said.

Sometimes his telephone rang in the night. She begged him to come at once. Her dreams were evil and overwhelming. Something threatened her. He would go cursing and muttering, driving on the wrong side of the road conscious of bad breath and aching eyes. When he got there he found the atmosphere freezing and vile and Beatrice cold with fear. Then he was brave. They sat it out with every light on while he calmed her, spoke with reason and humour exorcising the dreams. He held her until she was warm, put her to bed and lay beside her until her breathing told him she was asleep. He lay in the darkness and told himself that in the face of it all he was still a rational man. So he put it to me on that hot day in Charlotte Street.

At breakfast following such dramatic nights she was bright as a disc jockey while he sat silent. Another test passed. Another step towards—what? Death in a wooden house.

Part of the unspoken contract was that he should bear it alone. No heart to hearts with chums!

"Are you breaking the contract by telling me?"

He was startled. He had been silent for at least two minutes a very long time for him. I had taken him seriously. Uneasily he said, "It has changed. Something has happened."

That was the moment. Because of what I knew I thought that he was going on to tell me about the politics. About the company she kept now. I was completely wrong. My instinct said that suddenly he felt he could not trust me. I discovered from the first time I met him in Berlin that often I could either read his mind or accurately sense the drift of his thoughts when they concerned us both to the exclusion of everything else.

To test him I said, "E. M. Forster".

He laughed aloud, "Oh you sly peasant," he said, "yes, yes my dear fellow. Let's leave it at that!"

He remembered the day I had him round the throat and told him that they'd sent a hard man to feel my collar and I had not betrayed him because lads from my old *Alma Mater* the all-purpose village school ('I'll show you mine if you'll show me yours, give us a bunk up to look over the door of the girls' lavatory)— did not split on their mates. Well—not often.

It did not occur to me that it might be Beatrice, not myself, whom he suddenly distrusted.

It did not occur to me that whatever had happened to change their relationship hurt him so badly that he was grateful for what he took to be my understanding, my intuition, permitting him to leave it unsaid but sensed between friends.

Cheerfully he changed the subject. Paid the bill. Marched out into the street looking as if he should be put bodily into the nearest dry cleaner and given the heavy-stain treatment. I was so obtuse, believing myself distrusted, that I wanted to kick him. I had indigestion.

It was no time to tell him that on my recently-ended tour of duty in Belfast I served with the MRF. The Military Reconnaissance Force, known to the Provos as the Military *Reaction* Force. We wore plain clothes. We drove ordinary-looking cars. We were believed to be assassins.

We also took photographs.

At the anniversary of some Bloody weekday or other, outraged intellectuals, over from London on a day trip, marched courageously under the very muzzles of television cameras in Andersonstown. Giving, as they used to say in the old-fashioned shouting army, comfort to the enemy.

We took photographs. Two colleagues and myself.

There was one of Beatrice, two paces behind a famous actress, with her mouth open yelling a slogan. A handsome fellow at her elbow looked round for trouble. He was nearly as tall as the actress and his fair hair was groomed round his face covering his ears. He pointed at me and some lively buckos started to move in my direction to ask, no doubt, if they could look at my expensive camera because they admired it.

So the three of us got into our ordinary-looking car and drove peacefully away. We did not fail to change to another ordinary-looking car of a different colour and with different number plates the next day. We did not fancy being cut off in our prime. Or even a year or two later.

Three years later. Yesterday in London. To see Beatrice.

There is a lag in the mind, like jet travel in the body, when you remove from a place of violence that is familiar to a place where there is no violence.

The response to a sharp sound is out of proportion. The eyes glance above eye level, the body actually senses the open place and the place where the back is guarded, the hand does not reach out for the innocent thermos flask left on a window sill; wheel hubs, exhaust pipes, car doors a fraction open take the attention; the face of the smiling stranger about to ask the time, the direction, does not hold the gaze for above a tenth of a second, it is the position of the hands, the figure who might be the companion, the car in the background and above all the area *behind* that alerts every sense. The gun in the pocket does not seem superfluous.

Jack sat in a chair in Beatrice's office. Jack from Belfast to London. Disorientated. He sat with his back to the wall where he could see the door. He was not aware that he moved the small armchair to do this.

Jack watched Beatrice conduct her business.

Frank once quoted Sartre to Jack to illustrate the state of being *without* in every sense: "when the instruments are broken and unusable, when plans are blasted and effort is meaningless, the world appears with a childlike and terrible freshness suspended trackless in the void".

Jack had no plan. He had not considered what to say to Beatrice whom he had met only once, in Berlin. He felt without direction and purpose. He regarded Beatrice, and the other two women, as if they were inmates of a mental hospital. They seemed to him to suffer from the most dangerous of illusions—that their life had meaning and that they had control over their actions. They and everyone in the city round them.

The part of his mind that never went off duty told him that he was in a dangerous state. It knew the signs from other occasions. He was like an unstable explosive. He knew it. It took him unawares. It was not there when he got up, bathed, shaved, ate breakfast in his room, paid his bill, telephoned, made the appointment, walked all the way, pressed the bell, entered. It was then, immediately, there.

It was the impression she made on him.

He knew he must be as silent as possible, as still as possible and let it work its way through. As she continued her telephone marathon he considered the effect on a little Jewish boy of removing him suddenly from Nazi Germany; from a place of violence that is familiar to —— how many years, if ever, to achieve the transition? He was ashamed to make such a comparison and wondered if there should be, following the thousands of books, the trials, the testimonies, the film records—a silence. To permit the survivors and the children of the survivors to heal themselves.

The anger grew in him. He did not acknowledge it. He tamped it down. He would not permit the thought—how dare she laugh, joke, be provocative, how dare she not show sorrow, restraint. He had already decided that she had something to do with the death.

Could she really have been the object of Frank's passion as he described it? Was he blind? He was now. Jack had once looked down on him when he was drunk and asleep. His lips were slightly parted showing a little of the teeth as the dead show the teeth sprawled in the road with the eyes also partly open. This look of shock was appropriate.

Memory is not like an anchor chain, one solid link after another taking one down down out of the light. It is wayward. It is a labyrinth with its own rules. In quick succession two of the lies Frank told came to Jack's mind, he had never consciously thought them; it was not true that Frank's name, attached to his mother's name, was on the SS liquidation list; *he could never have seen it.* It was not true that he served in the army while the war was still on. *He was a year too young.* Why did he lie? To dramatize himself. To find some way, call it *artistic* truth, to present or to bear the intensity of his feelings, his sense of terror—in terms that would not frighten away those who had experienced neither. Signals, signals—listen to me, listen to me, like the old joke I'm not waving I'm drowning. Was suicide possible? Who would he want to punish as badly as that? Her? The one with the telephone on the long, long lead prowling the carpet in front of Jack?

The next thought shocked him. That his quest was not from friendship, from love, from gratitude. It was nothing but a monstrous conceit: Jack, the avenging hero. Now he has a peg on which to hang the story of his life which for all these years he has told himself making it more rich, more devious, more flattering on each of the thousand and one nights.

*   *   *

Frank had filled his pocket in the Italian restaurant with the wafers of peppermint chocolate they used to give you with the coffee. Walking up Charlotte Street he began to eat them greedily dropping the crinkled wrappers on the hot pavement as he went. After that he ate the Turkish Delights which he had lifted at the same time. His hands and jacket were powdered with them. All the time his eyes and nose streamed with hay fever.

Suddenly he said, "There is a South African."

"Oh?"

I wondered if he was referring to Jonathan's mistress and had forgotten (why should he remember after a decade or more?) that I was there when Renata spoke scathingly of the woman making him lose his temper.

"Yes. It gets more complicated all the time!—it's the son of Jonathan's mistress, you remember the scene we had with Renata in Berlin?"

"Hmm."

"At least," he said, "it is *not his son*."

Was that it? Was it really Jonathan's bastard by the lady. About to displace the faithful Frank. More jealousy?

"No?"

"Oh no," he said, "he would say. He never lies about things like that. The fellow is not Jonathan's son."

In Berlin Aunt Renata said, "Poor Stella", speaking of Jonathan's never-mentioned, overshadowed for a lifetime, wife. It is hard for the country boy remembering Chasser and Vera at Sunday dinner having a chuckle over something in the *News of the World* ("You put that *down*, Jack, you're too young for that, take it off him this minute, Charlie") to imagine a world where Jonathan, the rich solicitor, sits looking across the candles at the shadowy Stella and tells her he's just off to South Africa for a month or so with his mistress because Frank was saying, "Jonathan took her back to South Africa last year. A long, last, lingering sea voyage."

His tone was scathing and it did not change when he said, "She was dying of something or other unpleasant and wanted to go home and do it in style. An operatic end."

I had not realized he hated the woman. I wondered if Stella hated Jonathan that much.

"Frail she was," said Frank. "You never met did you?"

He knew perfectly well I had not met her. How irritating people of his sort are if you don't happen to love them. With their arrogant conventions of speech. "If I may?" they say meaning "I intend to whatever you may think" and "Do you see?" they say not giving a damn whether you do or not. Not that it was native to him, but like the Catholic convert he was extreme in his acquired way of life—the one place in the world where he felt safe and happy was Cambridge because he had gone to Kings and loved it, and one or two had loved him, and his precocious intelligence had been at full stretch. The style was his but in some sense he aped it. Jack should know. Jack had spent years climbing and changing. But Jack exuded irritation and moral judgements as he walked out of step with Frank in the streets west of the Tottenham Court Road. Stupid, sulking fool of a soldier.

"No, I never met her."

"Sensual and overblown. A prima donna always unwell with this or that—crying wolf, craving attention, *diminishing Jonathan.*"

"Has it ever occurred to you that Jonathan like a lot of other people does exactly what he wants and always has and therefore if he is being diminished he bloody well wants to be diminished!"

"What's the matter with you?"

"Nothing!"

There was dust blowing in the street. The habit of looking for trouble, for the glint on the gun barrel lifted the eyes to cramped rooms above shop signs: sweat shops for the rag trade—the last of the warrens where artists lived a century ago, you could see blue plaques on the wall here and there.

Men with long hair in nylon shirts, sweating white city faces, roll of fat over the trouser top, in and out the racks of dresses trollying along the pavements, slipping a back hander sometimes you just saw the notes as they went into the pocket—what for? To put the gear in the wrong van?

Hospital not far and ambulances turning in and one whole shop window ticking up on a huge graph the second by second increase in the world population—while I read it so many thousand babies stuck their heads out into the world and wished they hadn't. I wished they hadn't in the few seconds I bothered to consider it until the eye registered the latest scream on the news hoarding and went glazed.

Now I had put him off and he was sulking! Where shall we go? Across to the Trotskyite bookshop for light relief? Up and down the street past the uni-sex Sauna, is it a wanking parlour? And where do you hide your wallet? Up your orifice like convicts on Devil's Island? Their orifices must have been most marvellously flexible, perhaps they played tunes through them—trombone and tuba choruses, tympany on the chains. The bad temper did not ease. How dare he not trust me? The smell of the foods of five countries pumped out by extractors was like camels staling in your face as you went by. And over all the Post Office Tower stood sentry winking the aircraft clear.

Cordoned against bombers, of course. In every public London place blue men in white gloves searched your case, your handbag. Sometimes they missed something. The bang of disbelief, all round you in stopped time the wood and metal flying; you look down where your foot was, where your arm was; or you do not look because darkness has taken out your eyes. Sometimes what is left is put in plastic bags awash with heart's blood and they use buckets of water and yard brooms to clear the rest.

If you read of it you have only to turn the page of the paper and expunge it. But if you had been there recently as I had you cannot forget the sounds they make. And the smell. And after that he expected me to be *concerned* about the antics of little Jonathan and his mistress—the stuff on which middle-class literature and drama thrived? It would have cheered me to hear that Stella had stood up at last and used the bread knife on Jonathan. But I don't expect they had a bread knife. I expect it was electric.

"Go on," I said, "tell us some more—I'm bad tempered because I don't feel well."

Lies! Oh how trippingly they flow.

"Oh," he said, "so that's it! It never occurs to me that you are in anything but magnificent health."

"It wouldn't!"

"What's the matter?"

"A general malaise but not terminal."

"Well said; I'm glad that's come back."

"What?"

He pointed at the Post Office Tower.

"The mighty phallus in the sky. For years it was all tits. Marilyn ascendant. Mother Goddess on the rampage but it is back. Take heart! As I do seeing you again you Queen and Country Mastodon."

"So what is this about a South African?"

"Ah! Consider the dying mistress of my father. After so much crying wolf it answered and sank its teeth in. She was brave when she got the news. Bathos and courage in counterpoint. Imagine the farewells. What sunsets with black servants! Did you know that South Africa is so verdant so rich in some parts that there are two harvests in the year they do say? What a suitable irony that tyrants inhabit Eden. As for Peter her son—you can see why Jonathan agreed to bring him back—her last request. To take him into the practice. She obviously hoped he'd inherit. I don't envy the man as long as Jonathan is still true to Jonathan, taking in the strays. Look at me!" I stopped and looked at him. He was near to tears. Even then I was too dense to put out a hand to him. The second passed.

"The pollen this year," he said, "is of a virulence previously unknown. It is suggested that the Russians are dropping it from satellites!"

"What you need is a drink."

"They are closed."

"I have this bottle in my car."

"And where is that, dear heart?"

"In the park—are you fit to walk or have your legs atrophied with the decadent life you lead?"

"Lay on!"

We walked north through the old streets.

"Even if he were not on the make," said Frank, "I can understand that he and Beatrice would attract each other."

"Is he on the make?"

"Who isn't except Warrant Officer Jack?"

"You," I said, "and never have been."

"Ah!"

He would not let me see that my emphatic opinion pleased him. He was like Jonathan in that respect.

"He is younger you see; younger than she, that is. And she is now in that dangerous time for women, 33, 34 and ..." He hesitated and then, "and he is most attractively radical."

"Oh."

"Oh sure," he said, "speaks loud against the land of house arrest. But then who doesn't except the Monday Club?"

"What's he like?"

"Like?"

"Yes."

"Armchair revolutionary."

"Yes?"

"On committees. In with the Trots straight away."

"How do you know?"

"Beatrice."

"Her too?"

"Very stroppy about equal rights and all."

"Yes?"

"Yes."

"Oh."

"It doesn't mean anything, of course. Look at Jonathan! You'd expect her to be. And anyone Jonathan took on in the family as it were."

He started to laugh. "Do you remember Aunt Renata on the subject?"

"Yes."

"She had a remarkable effect on you."

"Yes. She opened my eyes as the saying goes."

"Berlin," he said, "Berlin, encircled, split in two by a wall. Symbol of schizophrenia. Flights to and from reality. That suited me. That suited me very well. Perhaps I should live there?"

"Don't ask me."

He looked at me reproachfully and said, "That was sharp, warrant officer, shall I now scrub out the latrines, sir?"

"Sorry."

We went north to the park. I looked inside and under the car before touching it. We sat on the grass with the bottle and regarded the boundary of the American ambassador's residence. It was more peaceful to look at than the zoo further on. No shots were fired and no one asked us what we were doing or to identify ourselves. We did not take that for granted any more.

"I don't think I can stay here in this country which I love and hate."

"What's happened?"

"Nothing. Something in the mind. Could I start again somewhere?"

"Sure."

"It's getting bad isn't it? Shall I be murdered in my generation as my mother was in hers?"

"Is that it?"

"Partly, partly."

"But you are not political. She was."

He looked sideways at me, sly; the way he could not help it. The look that told you he was treacherous against his will.

"That no longer applies, Jack."

"What are you mixed up with?"

"Nothing—I mean that like in my mother's time both the innocent and the guilty go down together."

Suddenly, irrationally it seemed, he burst out, "I have never forgotten what Renata said in Berlin; that at some time Jonathan would demand something of me as payment, as a right. It is disgusting. Utterly false to his character. It is I who try to express my gratitude. He cannot hear me. What is painful, what troubles me is that Renata was right about almost everything else even though I did not admit it at the time."

"How could you? She was knocking Jonathan. Also she loves you like a son and we all know about oedipus schmoedipus; so she is jealous not to have you for her own! Right?"

"How extraordinary," he said and he was tremendously cheered, "why you clever old sod, I never ever thought of her like that. I mean she always seemed beyond ignoble emotions! She's *jealous* of Jonathan that's it, my dear fellow; it warps her normally excellent mind. Do you know it has worried me on and off *for years*. Being my mother's sister. In some sense perhaps thinking of her as a mother, but not admitting it—well, well, well."

"This chap Peter," I said, "what does he look like?"

"Why?"

"I thought he might be one of your athletic, short back and sides."

"No no no—good lawyer; soft spoken, bit of a hypochondriac and very, very sharp under the hesitant smile."

Then he pointed at the girls walking in summer dresses and the men carrying their jackets.

"A bit like that," he said.

The one he aimed at was tall and his fair hair was carefully arranged round his head, covering the ears.

"I don't hate him," he said, "it's just that I don't see Bea very often now—but then."

He left it there and concentrated on the bottle.

Jack felt empty. And heavy. He made himself consider the scene before him in Beatrice's office. He fixed his face in a neutral expression and suppressed everything in his mind. In this way she would not pick up any signals, would not be alerted, would not think it necessary to be on guard.

Choose and act. Act and be free. Be free and do not regret the action. He had chosen to start with the belovéd sister. He was there, waiting. Waiting is part of action. He knew how to wait.

There were four telephones, two typewriters one of them electric with a jumping golf ball. The office was divided. The divider was elegantly designed part of it being a book case. Through the book case he could see parts of the other women as they moved, typed, answered the telephones. These parts of women were like pieces of a jig saw. One of them had beautiful breasts under a green silk blouse. The other had a grave and powerful profile reminiscent of Aunt Renata.

Beatrice moved continuously over the pile, amber, wall to wall. She wore a long skirt that reminded him of the Victorian tablecloth in his gran's cottage. It had a fringe with small soft bobbles and a nap he used to stroke at the same time moving his mouth rhythmically, sucking. It was red and black and orange and brown in an intricate pattern. So was Beatrice's skirt which she tucked up high between her legs when she sat suddenly on the carpet near him to continue her conversation. She was wearing black leather boots, high heels and very fine leather gripping the calf; were there garters above them like a tart in a Victorian knocking shop?

The other women sometimes answering two telephones at once, using the shoulder rests, spoke through the bookcase or sometimes came partly round the partitions (the grave profile was small with breasts like apples and an abundance of dark shining hair gathered round her head; the beautiful breasts were part of a more ample figure, a fair and smiling face; faithful women to Beatrice their leader and inspiration).

"It's Sybille."

"It's Christopher."

"It's Merlin."

"Can Mike have a word?"

"For you."

"For you, Bea."

"I have a note in the diary."

"I can order a car."

Beatrice covered the mouthpiece of her telephone, it was clearly the command telephone because it was scarlet and had a dial in its base.

"I'll ring him back."

"I'm not here, I'm in a meeting."

"The photographs will be ready today, put him on to Arnold."

"I won't agree the cheque for a thousand until I have the guarantee, he knows that, refer him to —— "

"Tell . . . no you can do that the file is over there."

"It can't be Tuesday and Wednesday is Woman of the Year lunch, so try for . . . you have the diary."

"Yes I'll speak to him."

Now she had two telephones and a notebook. She wrote back-sloping, large on the page. She had hands and wrists like a small man and wore a watch with a wide strap.

Was the atmosphere of tension, the slight edge of hysteria an everyday part of her business? What was her business? Jack never decided.

On the wall were paintings. They were savage in colour and feeling. There was a tangible effect from them. They jarred the mind. They were violent. They reminded him of bomb blasts in shopping centres.

The grave profile brought him coffee, but first she brought coffee to Beatrice and was solicitous of her murmuring something to her with her face averted from Jack and then going into another room to fetch a small bottle, a tiny bottle that Jack not looking anywhere near it saw contained minute white tablets. Beatrice took two, discreetly, and touched the hand that had brought them. But Jack was politely reading one of a pile of expensive and colourful magazines on a polished table beside him. In one of them was a full-page advertisement for a scent for young women to wear in the folds of the vagina or their lovers would be repelled.

Beatrice once more on the move pushed her hand through her short tight-curled copper hair (in Berlin it was black, to the shoulder) and sometimes made a conspiratorial face at him (she had fine large eyes), as she talked, and talked and talked. Sometimes she made expressive and large movements and in mid-gesture seemed to be taken by the elegant way her wrist turned and her free hand hung suspended. Sometimes she took the large stone set in a ring on her forefinger between her lips and gently pressed it, wetting it, looking at Jack as she did so. Sometimes she dealt with the telephone lead as a singer deals with the lead of a hand microphone making the movement part of the performance.

Jack waited. Beatrice had a special voice for men on the telephone. It suggested dark honey. She had another voice for women and her expression changed. She no longer smiled showing her small white nipping teeth. Her tone was sharp. The change was unconcealed and instant. The mouth, fleshy when smiling and wide, contracted and thinned. Jack had noticed none of this in Berlin.

She caught him looking, shrugged and when for a moment she was not on the telephone she said, "You're so quiet, Jack. What happened to you? You were so *eager* in Berlin, Frank used to do imitations of you. Like a boy scout with a banner with your passion for *England* and the future. Onwards and upward. It made them all laugh, and the way you sat and sucked it all in, all that refugee rubbish, you know Edward's dead don't you?"

"Is he?"

"I thought you were in touch with Frank."

"Not much."

"Your voice has changed too. You had a rather fetching country voice."

"Have you changed, Beatrice?"

"Call me Bea. I expect so. Excuse me."

As she began another call she went to the bookcase and took a small book from it and handed it to him. Before she spoke on the telephone she said, "Sign it while you're here—you never know you may be worth something at some time."

For a moment there was a glinting look in her eye and she seemed as she moved to be on heat.

"It's surprising," she said although the person on the other end of the telephone was already speaking and she covered the mouthpiece, "how clearly I remember you—perhaps what I remember is Frank's version of you? I was even a bit jealous of you."

Jack held the book without opening it. The younger woman leaving all the telephones to the older, began to fold about 300 single sheets of paper with some message or statement roneoed on them and place them in buff envelopes. She had to kneel on the floor to do this. She had a machine with a roller and water to stick the envelopes. Each envelope had a little white square with an address on it. Jack averted his eyes from the green silk blouse. Perhaps he too was on heat.

Jack offered to help. Beatrice who seemed to have been concentrating on her call said at once, "No she can do it."

The fair and smiling woman turned her face to Jack to thank him. He went back to his small armchair. It was covered with a slippery material, each time he leaned back he slid forward.

The central heating oppressed him. The necessity for lights to be on in the middle of the day oppressed him. The absurdity of the situation oppressed him. The stage beyond absurdity is action.

I opened the book. It had been published over a decade earlier. Another world. Sergeant Pepper's world. When Frank was staying at Cambridge.

It was the only place in England he was really happy. Near his old college. When he met me at the station I told him how cheerful he seemed, even healthy; he said, "I'm Peter bloody Pan and Wendy is a transvestite don from Magdalen who fancies his chance at theatricals and has an almost feminine partiality for old china —so show us your hook, Captain, and watch out that one of the local crocodiles doesn't bite it off for you; if you've improved your table manners —— "

"*My* table manners."

"I'll wangle you in where I have dining rights and you can see how the mad, the gay, the extraordinarily crafty and self-seeking and one or two who are actually brilliant conduct themselves—I refer to the high table, no less. Tell them, if asked, that you are in Intelligence—they won't believe anyone who is in Intelligence would *say* he was in Intelligence but with your quiet sincerity."

"My *what*?"

"Your way of looking through one, yes you do, after that they will be intrigued even amused by anything else you say even though they have a frightfully low opinion of everything except themselves. It *is a pleasure* to gaze upon your honest and home-spun countenance, sergeant, you are a sergeant now?"

"Yes since —— "

"It worries me, it's like the policemen; you look far too young for it. And we all know what that means. It means poor old Frank is over the hill —— "

"Poor old Frank!"

"Enough of that! And don't worry, pretty as you are you won't be molested even by the oldest of fruits because they'll accept that you're mine all mine and that I've been slumming again."

"What a charming way to put it."

"I thought you'd like that."

"Please do not run over that cyclist, Franky."

"I only do that on Tuesdays. Are you hungry?"

"Very."

"There's a pub by the river would suit you."

"Oh?"

"Touch of the Rupert Brookes. It will appeal to your romantic nature. Not only that it's cheap."

It was early summer. Uncertain weather. Meadows and river; bridges and colleges; Japanese tourists, bookshops and pubs. If you are clever you can have all this. Drink beer, lean on the parapet, watch the water cascade over the weir and the mishandled punt go broadside. I was not much older than the fellows I was looking at. With their girls.

Frank had an I-told-you-so look in his eye.

"Ah my dear boy," he said looking sly, "look what you missed! That serves you right for being born a peasant in a village and why, I ask myself, are you not a militant trades unionist attempting to get your own back? Come to think of it you are extraordinarily deficient in class feelings. What frees you from this English obsession?"

"Well," I said, "I mean ter say, Franky, like, I'm a natural haristocrat en I, eh? I mean my dad's granny got shafted by the squire's wicked son diden she, poor old cow, so there's blue blood in me en there makes me rise above your ordinary pig-ignorant working feller?—ho yerse—wot you see before you is definitely not rubbish, mate."

"My boy my boy," he said in his Jewish delicatessen-owner's voice, "I can see we shall get on. Come on a week's trial for no money."

They looked like kings those undergraduates to Jack leaning on the parapet of a bridge looking down at them. But how many of them could write poetry?

Not long before this Cambridge day Jack had been in Cyprus. Peace-keeping with the UN. The blood of Jack's mate was all over a café wall one afternoon. He failed to duck the cross fire. Jack's girl at home when she heard told him he had to stop soldiering and buy himself out or they were finished. And so they finished and Jack missed her because Jenny was a gentle girl and loved him more that he deserved or had realized.

After the death of his mate and the parting of his girl it came over him to write the poems. They concerned his village. And love. And death. Of course!

There was a lad in the village, Brian, loved a girl when he was seventeen. She left him. He did it in style. The motor bike was on HP. Over the ton to oblivion. Builder's labourer was Brian, strong in the arm, filthy tongue ("Wash your mouth out with soap and water this minute, you dare say that word in front of me!") and ignorant as a pig. Pity to say Pig. Pigs are clean animals.

There he was loving ignorant pig down the graveyard across the main road from the village, in his box in his big, black polished car the only time he ever rode in one of those. Artificial grass spread over the mud; and the man in the black coat putting in two separate finger fulls of grey powder, "ashes to ashes" flick went the two fingers, "dust to dust" flick went the two fingers as the vicar brayed. The black-coat man from the Co-operative Funeral Department, he bowed his head and dusted his fingers and his four lads, also black coats, got back in the car thinking Brian had

123

been heavy. The Co-op was the cheapest for funerals. Did they give their divi stamps with the service? The RIP divi, to stick in a book? To Brian's parents who would never have believed it if Jack told them why Brian did it.

But all the lads knew. All the lads felt the same. Didn't Jack feel the same when he went for a soldier because his first girl the tomboy lay out in the fields with the soldier? Romeo wasn't a freak and he wasn't Italian. He was Jack and Brian and the rest beside. For a short season. Of course if she hadn't left him and they'd wed he'd have knocked her about, betrayed her, worn her down. We all do one way or another, don't we?

So thought Jack, and when they were finished he sent the poems to Frank. Thirty of them. The first being called "Brian to Oblivion".

Brian's girl cried and cried in the village church so that everyone noticed her.

We walked along the Backs. English flowers, places where flood water had receded, sudden showers of rain—how *detached* it was. Frank beside me with stubble on his face and a faint smell of sweat coming off him. He had grown his hair a little to be in the fashion. And he wore zip-sided boots. I talked to him about Jenny. I was surprised how much it seemed to affect me seeping through bit by bit over a long time.

"She thought I might get shot in the back; if not Cyprus somewhere else."

"You might."

"True."

"Save you growing old and decrepit, blocked waterworks —— "

"Grandad's got an anal stricture!"

"Ah! You're getting quicker."

"Or are you getting slower?"

"Now that's *wicked*!"

"You'll worry about that, won't you?"

"I have to wear glasses to read, now! and —— "

"Serves you right, it's all that sex."

"Oh do you think so?"

"Of course it is, Frank—everyone knows that!"

"My God! It'll be herbs and spells next—it is *simply elasticity* ask any ophthalmic surgeon?"

"Surgeon? What's wrong with an occulist—you're not going blind or something are you?"

"Of course not—it is mainly after meals I need my glasses."

He was concerned. I could see that.

"What are they like?"

"What?"

"Your specs?"

"Like any others of course."

"Put them on."

"No! Not out here."

"Go on, Franky, show us—give us a treat."

"I could not make up my mind, so in the end I settled for John Lennon."

He put on the steel-rimmed spectacles and glared at me. I howled with laughter and he took them off. He was furious.

"It wasn't them," I said unable to stop laughing, "it was you. Put them on again."

"Don't be a prick."

"Go on—you silly vain sod, put 'em on."

He did. He looked like my brother Ben used to look when he was five and his specs too large for him. He looked very sharp peering through them as if ready to bite the leg of the school doctor. Frank I mean.

"Great," I said, "it gives you style and authority."

"Do you think so?"

"Yes."

"Not reminiscent of Himmler?"

"With all that hair? More like a senior psychiatrist."

"Oh really?"

"Really. I'd think twice before I tried to put it across you in those specs, mate, I tell you."

"You sure?"

"Certain."

"Oh good," he said quite seriously, "I'd worried about that. Of course they are only for reading."

He put them away.

"You'll come to it, Jack! Take my tip and hold out as long as you can. I mean even if you have to prop the book up on the other side of the room."

"Right you are, Skip."

For once there seemed no hurry. On that day on the bank of the Cam. Except that I hoped fairly soon he would say something about the poems.

He was smiling round him. He really loved it, every brick and stone, every court and notice and that included a battle between two punt crews. One lot went into the water and made a point of putting their funny hats on to swim ashore. One of them was in white tie, tails and a topper.

"Do you know what they do after this, Jack?"

"Rule the world?"

"They go into their fathers' businesses most of them."

"They should be so lucky."

"Lucky! My dear boy! The rest of your life in the city or the Civil Service or . . . I mean classics on the floor of the Stock Exchange do you imagine? The Icelandic sagas on the 8.15 from Bromley? All they do here is stock up and hope it will last the rest of their lives. Do you know what most of them are reading at 40?"

"Tell me and I'll pass it on to the Ford workers, they could do with a new idea or two."

"Thrillers, and doing *The Times* crossword, dear heart; now about those poems of yours."

He nearly caught me which he meant to but I kept looking at the river. He did not sound quite as confident as usual so I braced myself for the let-down.

"It pains me to say, Jack, being, as I am, a well-known retarded student type from the very pages of *The Cherry Orchard* and ever, myself, about to write, as you will remember, my masterpiece concerning The Chosen Race in the style of the great Heller—it pains me, I repeat, to say to an old friend who has actually put pen to paper—that the poems are rather *good!*"

I felt wonderful. I nearly jumped in the river. I looked sideways at him. He was looking sideways at me, sly as ever. He started to smile and so did I and then we laughed; and it got out of control and I laughed and laughed until tears ran down my face at the best joke I ever heard and I got hold of him and shook him and embraced him and he hated every minute of it and swore at me until I stopped.

"I shall call you Captain Id, after this," he said. "My God you spare us nothing in the way of violent feelings in your verse. No wonder you joined the army. I never understood it before. You wouldn't be *safe* in normal life."

"But none of them is about me. I wouldn't do that."

"All of them are about you, my friend—and it's better out than in! How much *lighter* you must feel."

"Only because you say so. That makes me feel very good."

He began to play an invisible violin which sufficiently deflated me.

We wandered off to his room. It was a guest room up a lot of stairs under a sloping roof. His clothes and books were everywhere and a pile of pirate records in plain sleeves from a company he was involved with run by Boris in America. Boris had given up silence and settled to taping, illegally, great performances in the concert hall and the opera house (he had contacts in Italy and Germany as well) and pressing and distributing them. Frank was involved in order to preserve recordings of works that the musicians union would inexorably destroy after 21 years. Frank also specialized in persuading broadcasting companies in Germany and Holland to lend him recordings of historic performances which he taped overnight and returned the next day. As we entered he was telling me that the archives of the BBC are the hardest to crack. He spoke affectionately of the new, commercial Boris who sent a monthly newsletter full of the most intimate details of Boris's exotic life, and a list of the latest records for sale. The company was called Eureka Records. Frank was not too keen on that.

As we negotiated his gear, and moved things to find a place to sit he said, "I consider it my public duty to preserve great voices, great performances, and that concludes the case for the defence, your honour—oh! and by the way, Jack, would you mind signing one or two of these while you are here?"

I thought it had something to do with Eureka Records. He had just removed a wet towel, a pair of trousers and one shoe from a small table top to show a pile of books some toppled over, some still contained within an opened cardboard box. They were obviously all the same thing. About the size of an exercise book, thin with a brilliant green cover on which there was bold printing in black type. He handed one to me. I could smell its newness.

I was stupefied. I read the title *Brian to Oblivion* and under it my name. I could not comprehend it. I opened it. I let the pages turn. The poems were beautifully laid out on the thick white paper. He had paid to have them privately printed. I kept picking up copies and putting them down.

Just in case I embarrassed him further Frank gave an invisible gun belt a hoist round an invisible fat belly and let rip in the high snickering whinny of the unique Andy Devine, "Aaaaaaaaaaaaaaaw shucks, Frankee boy! Why in hell did ya hev ta go en do thet fur? Throwin' away yer money like a danged fule on a bunch of sissy pomes. Aaaaaaaaaaaam ashamed of ya."

Jack sat in the shiny chair with the copy that Beatrice had handed him. He signed it under the title inside. There was an inscription from Frank to Beatrice. As he read it he heard Frank say, "How did we suddenly come to it, Beatrice and me? After knowing each other a lifetime?"

There is a moment for it—when the one is ready for the other, when the sum of each at that time, and time is everything, makes the attraction irresistible. Time and chance. Chance that they will be in each other's orbits at that time.

Beatrice was off the telephone. She talked to visitors. He shut out the conversations, the falsities of smile and touch. He sat like a lead buddha unable to find the key to his being there. In the most inaccessible part of his mind (hindsight it has to be, but how else to convey the atmosphere?) a tiny recurring flicker of instinct signalled "wrong wrong wrong—something is wrong".

It was not the red warning; merely a nagging distracting sense of going wrong. In every move she made, every word she uttered, there was the lie to Frank's description of their liaison. This woman had suffered no recent loss (two months only—two short months) of a lover who had for years steered her away from the borders of madness; calmed her primitive fears for transgressing tribal laws of incest.

The hysteria was there, of course, in the vibrating self-regard, the posturing, the abrupt changes of tone. But not sadness. Not pain and loss. The child caught in the act freezes looks straight at you does not blink. Would run but you block the way. Stares you out. Defies you by its attitude. That was it. Already Jack had sat waiting for two and a half hours (on the telephone she said, "Come round, now—I have an easy morning").

But to what end? Was it deliberate or part of something else? Passing him she tapped the book and said, "That was a nice little five-finger exercise in its way. Did you ever go further and try the real thing. Some real writing?"

"I think I will," said Jack ignoring the intended insult.

"You must let me see it."

"Why?"

"You would if it were Frank wouldn't you?"

"If it were Frank."

"Oh I see."

When he first came in she said, "I think you've got bigger and you don't look like a bumpkin any more."

"Oh."

For a moment the glinting randy look was in her eye as she summed him up. Then she said, "I suppose you know about Frank?"

"Yes I heard."

"It was terrible," she said, "sit over there and read a magazine."

He watched them end the morning's . . . what? Work would you call it? Activity. The morning's activity dwindled. The telephones stopped ringing. Outside the windows the sky was so heavy it seemed already lighting-up time. The last visitor was flattered through the door. The older woman moved so discreetly that Jack missed her going. He helped the younger to balance a cardboard box in her arms with the 300 envelopes to go to the post office. He considered going with her. This may have shown in his face because when he closed the door behind her and turned to Beatrice she said, "I think I'll sack that girl; there is only one Queen Bee in this establishment."

He smiled. She did not smile.

"Why did you 'phone me?" she said.

"An impulse, really."

"Would you like a drink?"

"Fine."

"Whisky?"

"Beer?"

"In the fridge out here—I'll just —— "

She went through to the far side of the room divider and into another room.

Jack heard the faint snick of a key into the lock of the front door. He moved without thought out of the line of fire and was in a position to kill the intruder before the door was opened.

The tall, fair-haired man whom Jack had last seen pointing towards him in the Belfast demo three years earlier came into the room. When he became aware of Jack he did not seem surprised. But there was no flicker of recognition. When taking the photographs Jack wore spectacles with plain glass, and an ordinary cloth cap. His suit was nothing you would notice, mid-brown and off the cheapest peg, on those patrols.

At the moment of seeing him the man was calling "Bea! Bea!" He smiled at Jack and made no attempt to introduce himself. He wore jeans manufactured to look faded in patches and a bright, flower-pattern shirt. His leather coat cut like a reefer hung round his shoulders with the sleeves dangling. It had a fur collar. You could see the gold chain round his neck but not the cross or whatever it was on the end. He wore cowboy-type boots in soft fine leather with tall heels.

He was five years younger and six inches taller than Beatrice who came back with opened beer cans. She put them down and kissed him and Jack now knew why he had been kept waiting. The son of Jonathan's mistress of whom Frank spoke so scathingly was here for moral support. Peter, the bright young solicitor (solicitor? in those clothes? It was hard to take seriously in those clothes, and the hair arranged so carefully round the head over the ears. But look at the eyes. They don't look at you. And the whole attitude so casual. What is he full of? Not the obvious—but cotton wool? marshmallow? Don't be deluded)—who is going to inherit Beatrice *and* Jonathan's firm.

"Peter this is Jack."

"Hallo."

"Hallo."

"Jack was a friend of Frank's in Berlin."

"In Berlin!"

As if he did not know from her telephone call before Jack arrived!

"Yes, I was for a bit."

"Jack is a soldier."

"No I'm not," said Jack in a surprised voice and beamed at them both, "not for years. I lead a useful life now."

"But I thought —— "

"Short service, you see."

"There was that letter, you remember, Peter, when we were going through Frank's things?"

Jack for the first time that day is alive—Jack's mind goes into top gear from a standing start. Letter, Frank? *That one.* What did it say? Will they still have it for reference? Not likely, not at all likely? Written from where? Yes. From home. Before going back to Belfast. No army address. "Yes I remember," said Peter and the faintest trace of South Africa underlay his accent, "you said you were on leave."

"To do with your parents," said Beatrice.

"It's funny how you still use the old army expressions," said Jack drinking his beer, "and I was very upset. I was over to bury my parents after an accident."

Some people might have expressed conventional regret. These two did not waste the time.

"Over?" said Peter.

"Over," said Jack helpfully, "so I thought I'd try to contact old Frank. I telephoned his number two or three times but he wasn't there so I dropped him a line. I was sorry to miss him."

"Yes," said Beatrice, "he was away about that time; I mean it was just before he died."

"Away," said Jack, "ah! well I tried."

No one seemed to have anything else to say. Jack knew from experience that the information you extracted seemed more satisfactory than the information volunteered. It gave the questioner a sense of superiority. Jack looked ruefully at Peter. Jack seemed at a loss to be there with two such sophisticated people. Jack's attitude was that of the soldier invited to have a drink in an officer's house after an afternoon's cricket. It invited the host to make small talk to relieve the uneasiness of the guest. And feel free to ask questions. It disarmed.

131

"Well," said Peter, "you didn't pick very good weather when you made the journey."

"No," said Jack.

"Just now you said you were over—from somewhere?"

"America."

"America," said Beatrice, "well!"

"Yes," said Jack, "when my parents were killed, you see. My brother sent me a cable."

"But that was, what? Two months ago?"

"Oh yes. Yes it was."

"And you've been here ever since?" said Peter.

"Oh no." Jack sounded slightly put out.

There was a type of thick-headed innocent suspect who, when you interrogated him, actually lost his temper when you asked him simple questions to establish his movements; after all if he knew with certainty what he had been doing it must be obvious to everyone else, so why are you asking stupid questions? Jack presented a modified version of this attitude to Peter. Peter was charmingly persistent. It was not difficult to respond. The quality, common to confidence tricksters and lechers of seeming to be deeply absorbed in the victim, to be interested and admiring, came naturally to him. A beguiling man.

"Good lord," said Peter, "to and from America twice in such a short time? An expensive business nowadays."

"Well," said Jack, "well!" Obviously he was flattered.

"Whereabouts in America?"

"What?" said Jack.

"Do you live?" asked Peter, "let me top you up, not bad beer this."

"Dayton, Ohio," said Jack who by now had time to remember the main points of his brother's newsletter.

Ben had taken well to the American way of life. Three times a year he wrote a long report which began "Dear Friends". It was magnificently duplicated and sent to all from the barest acquaintance to the closest relations with a short, handwritten paragraph at the end to prove that Ben still remembered which of them was which. Jack received the most recent one on the same day as the anonymously posted newspaper cutting which reported Frank's death.

"Oh really," said Peter, "Ohio."

"I'm a dental technician," said Jack, "they pay, they really pay for that kind of service over there. Although I have to tell you that pricewise things over here are just as —— "

"Everybody says it," remarked Beatrice who was bored and looking at her watch.

"Ohio?" said Peter as if groping for some piece of information just out of reach, "Dayton?"

"Near Cleveland. Up by the great lakes."

"Of course it is!"

"Have you been there?"

"No," said Peter, "but we have a client. He is over at the moment."

"Oh really?"

"They have a newspaper with a title that always attracted me?" said Peter, "you must know it. It's the daily Cleveland newspaper. Now what is it? It's on the tip of my tongue, as they say."

In the silence Beatrice no longer looked at her watch. Jack let it hang while he drank half his beer, smiled at them to show he enjoyed it, put the glass down and then blew his nose.

"The newspaper," he said.

"Yes," said Peter, "surely you know it?"

"Oh you mean *The Plain Dealer*," said Jack.

"So I do," said Peter, "isn't it fun? A title like that for a republican paper."

"When you speak to your client," said Jack, "you ask him if he supports the Cleveland orchestra, we do; it's truly wonderful to go there all winter."

"I'm sure he does," said Peter. But still he was doubtful.

Jack thought, it's the clothes, my clothes; they don't tie-up. All bought in England. That's why he's got sharper.

"Yes," said Peter, "he's a rich fellow; we have to look after some rich fellows in order to defend poorer fellows."

"Good for you," said Jack enthusiastically, "and I'll bet he lives in Shaker Heights, doesn't he?"

"Yes he does," said Peter, "how clever of you."

"No," said Jack, "all the rich nobs live there—millionaires corner. I expect he knows . . ." and Jack listed two or three tycoons who benefited from brother Ben's dentures, inlays and bridges.

Part of the tri-annual report always read like a prospectus for Ben and Family Inc, and listed Ben's achievements. Jack suddenly realized he did not like Ben very much. He forgot Peter and Beatrice because he remembered how much Vera had worried and cared for Ben and his terrible eyesight, and how Chasser had sweated to earn extra to kit Ben out for grammar school so he wouldn't look a poor kid. Hearts and flowers, Frank would have said, but sod Frank for the moment and all rich, or well-off, sons of bitches on both sides of the Atlantic; and sod Ben for not coming to the funeral to see Vera and Chasser off properly. Fresh anger combined with the anger suppressed all the morning was aimed like a laser at Peter who was so easy, and whose skin was so well kept and who smelled, faintly, of expensive soap and after-shave and cigars, and at Beatrice both of whom, it seemed, were deeply concerned with robbing the rich to defend the poor as long as it didn't put them out at all.

He remembered Frank saying, "He is fashionably radical". Radical! Radical! Neither of them had ever seen a hungry child except on television, never heard a shot fired, never smelled the stench of poverty, never been pissed over by a half-wit in an adventure playground, never carried a bedpan in a hospital ward, never been down a mine or a sewer or driven a bus for eight hours or delivered mail at six on a wet morning or been homeless and without any prospect and separated from those they love, never —oh Jesus Christ! and all the morning she and those visitors, those 'phone conversationalists! their dreadful miseries like the increased charges to have their big motor cars serviced, and the crippling rent for their four telephone extensions and the delay in delivery of . . . never mind, never mind, this is not the object of the exercise. Hold to the action. Action is freedom. It's nearly time to spring the cutting on them. Perhaps that will disturb his lovely demeanour; I'll bet he's wonderful on committees, even in those clothes.

"I must ask him," said Peter politely. He was convinced.

"Not," said Jack modestly, "that they would know me—I work for a group of four dental surgeons. Someone sent me this, by the way."

They took it, each holding a corner. They bent over it their heads touching. They read it as if they had never seen it before.

Peter took longer to read it than Beatrice. They did not seem to want to hand it back. Jack reached out and put it in his pocket.

"I wondered how you knew," said Peter, "having had no reply to your letter."

"Yes," said Jack, "otherwise I couldn't, could I? No one else wrote to me."

"What about it?" asked Beatrice.

"There was a letter with it," lied Jack, "anonymous."

"Have you got it?" asked Peter.

"Not with me."

"What did it say?"

"You see," said Jack, "just after I finished tidying up my parents' affairs I got the letter and the cutting. I had to go back to Dayton and it started to worry me. And we always intended to have a family Christmas in England, you don't get panto for the kids in America it's all telly telly telly and *Amahl and the Night Visitors*, you know don't you, so the wife said, 'Jack, why don't we go this year and then you can ask about your friend, and very soon it might not be safe to visit England anyway the way things are going over there,' so we decided to do that and that's why—you see?"

"Not quite," said Peter.

"It said in the letter," said Jack, "that it was political. It said Beatrice would know."

"I certainly do not know."

"Oh?"

"I'm sorry you didn't bring that letter, Jack. Although I'm surprised you should pay any attention to an anonymous message."

"Well, Peter, you see at first I didn't. And then I said to myself someone has taken the trouble to find my address. And whoever it is knows I owe Frank a lot. And then I remembered something."

"What was that?"

"Frank never took drugs."

Peter was excellent. He smiled and then he laughed. He took Jack's arm in the friendliest way and said, "My dear fellow you are behind the times in Dayton, Ohio—nearly everyone takes something—do you *know* the figures for sleeping pills and tranquillizers over here? And pot? Not so much the hard stuff but ... I mean most of my best friends, as they say."

Jack did not reply.

"Nearly everyone takes something nowadays!"

"Are they pushers?"

"What?"

"Are they pushers? Your best friends?"

"I doubt it."

"We know a lot about them even in Dayton, Ohio."

"I suppose you do but I don't see —— "

"If you're right there has to be a pusher, I thought I might look for him."

"What?"

"Who died with Frank?"

Beatrice said, "I don't want to talk about it any more, do you mind? I'm sorry Peter but we've had a terrible morning, crisis after crisis, and I don't want to."

"Oh sorry," said Jack, "I thought you were over it; you didn't seem bothered when we talked about him earlier. So sorry."

"I was *shattered*. I had to go to a health farm to recover. It cost a fortune. I had to have complete rest. I was unbelievably *fragile* for weeks. How dare you say —— "

"Sorry. So sorry."

"It's all right Bea."

"But what is he suggesting, Peter? I mean it's not all right."

"I'll push off now," said Jack, "I've rented a car. I shall just drive down there and have a look round."

There was a silence. Beatrice lit a French cigarette the sort Frank smoked.

"Down where?" said Peter as if he didn't know.

Jack took the cutting from his pocket.

"Down there. Just to look round. I think I'll get a little buddy buddy with the local coppers and perhaps take the chap who wrote this for a drink. Just to satisfy myself, Peter."

"But Jack—Frank is dead, the matter is closed."

"Yes but you see, Peter, they have this feeling in America, you know—the way they finally got to Nixon in the end. I mean a citizen must speak out. Frank never took drugs. I expect Beatrice and Jonathan didn't know that or they'd have said so at the inquest. If I'm wrong—what changed him?"

"What the hell has it to do with you," said Beatrice, "you stupid, self-satisfied boy scout. Keep your nose out of my family—it has been terrible enough without you stirring. Go back to America where they shoot innocent students, Kent State is Ohio isn't it? A citizen must speak out! My God, in a corrupt capitalist society and smug little reactionaries like you —— "

Peter stopped her by holding her.

"Why don't you leave us alone for a minute, Bea? Would you do that, please. I don't think Jack intends to upset you. And you know he was very fond of Frank."

"No," she said, "no."

She moved away from them to look out of the window.

"What are you up to, Jack?"

"I told you."

"Suppose, for a moment, there was something about Frank's death that was not reported. Had it occurred to you it might be to his discredit?"

"No."

"And that his family might be protecting him."

"But he is dead so it would not matter to him."

"It matters to them."

"Yes," said Jack, "I can see that."

He might have left it there but she turned on him from the window and said, "Christ he had terrible taste; who are you anyway? An ignorant conceited soldier he picked up in Berlin to amuse himself—and this" she strode to the shelves and took out the book of poems, "it's embarrassing. The slim volume published by the poet's friend. My *dear!*"

Jack walked to the door.

Peter said, "Just a minute" and put out a hand to restrain him. Jack froze and said, "I'm going now. Thank you for seeing me."

Peter was confident because he topped Jack by inches. And he was used to getting his own way.

"Don't be silly," said Peter, "have another beer."

He attempted to bring Jack back into the room.

Jack opened his mouth and shouted "No!" and as he did so he back handed Peter across the face knocking him the width of the room to fall over the armchair. Beatrice screamed and then stopped as Jack stepped towards her. He took the book of poems from her hand and tore it in two in four in eight and let it fall across the thick pile of the carpet.

"How dare you not mourn him! He adored you, you voracious bitch."

She went to Peter to comfort him. He sat in the armchair. His nose bled. Jack left them.

V I

I SAT IN the car and considered the day. The rain hammered the roof and poured down the windows. Dipped headlights wavered in the streams of water; from the branches of the tree overhead water sluiced down at intervals sounding on impact like wet concrete hitting the car.

Suitable weather. The park police patrols were out saying the gates will close in a quarter of an hour. Somewhere over in the teeming darkness of late afternoon deer were getting the washdown of their lives.

After Beatrice I sought and found Renata. After that for some primitive reason I went north to Stamford Hill. I drove past it twice. I had never seen the house before. It was hard to believe that there the Jewish refugee stood resolutely by the door until his saviour came home each day, and there the little dark girl adored the awkward unpredictable boy. Frank once spoke of decoding stones. I would have been glad to decode that house. To regret an action is a betrayal of freedom. Dogma. I sat betraying freedom. At least the golden boy from South Africa had spoken. They feared an enquiry. They feared some shame. Well, it would come back to Jonathan soon enough. So let Jonathan come to me.

And I had seen Renata. "She is in the book," said Beatrice during morning coffee. "God knows why she wastes money on a telephone in her position." I have not cried since I was fifteen and they scrubbed me. But I could cry for Renata in her wheelchair. I had not eaten. My head ached. I never had delusions of being superman. I have seen too many go down. Man lives not by logic but by Russian roulette. Blessed is he who does not know the difference.

I drove out of London.

The turn off the motorway was not familiar. The bad, winding road was not familiar. But at the intersection with the lights, where the old Roman road still ran, the mill stood with a single sail and holes smashed in the walls. It came back to me. I once brought

Frank to Battletown by this turning. We came through the Medway towns. *That* was the day he had the row in the teashop at Chatham and shouted and stammered. Of course! But when? It was the old Ford Popular, still? Yes. It must have been the first time I saw him in the UK after I came home from Berlin. Bored he was and I told him about the holiday that Festival of Britain summer when Ben and I saw the sea for the first time and nagged (Vera speaking) our parents sick to live in Battletown forever— or at least the next month whichever was longer.

"Take me there immediately," he said.

So I did. Nowhere to pull over and think until outside the new town, with the blue lights round the factories and the amber strips flaring up to the sagging dirty sky, there was a transport caff. Container lorries that later I heard shake the walls of The Battle Flag had cut trenches in the mud of its parking area.

I had a bacon-and-egg sandwich and tea made with caustic soda. But I could not recall the day we came down. Only the row en route. And something about the continental ferry. I had a very clear picture of our standing and watching it dock in front of The Battle Flag. I know, from being told, that the place had already turned to something dreary, but not yet derelict, evocative—at that time.

One other thing Gwen told me. That her auntie had a stall above the shingle beach in those hopeful, never-had-it-so-good, days. At the weekends she helped her serve the day trippers. So, more likely than not, we crunched along to buy ice cream in cornets, candy floss even, because Frank could never have tasted candy floss at public school and Kings!

But Jack did not notice the young woman, and the young woman did not notice Jack. Because, as with Frank and Beatrice, it was not yet their time.

Their time will begin tomorrow, on a day after the rain, when she will knock on the door of the hotel room and say, "Sorry if I'm interrupting but you left this in the shop and you paid for it and here's your change as well".

Jack will say, "That is very kind of you" and take the paperback and the money; she will come into the room. They will both be aware that the hotel is empty and still. When Jack says, "Would you like a cup of tea?" and she says, "Yes that would be nice if

I'm not interrupting", he will reach out to help her take off her coat. As he does this she will respond immediately, mistaking his gesture, by opening her arms to him. He will pause for what seems a century and she will begin to draw back and then they will embrace feeling as if they have the whole of time before them. Chance is sometimes a very fine thing.

The night before we met I lay alone in the great bed where admirals and their women had lain before me. The wooden shutters were folded out across the windows and held in place by their metal bars. The sign with the red flag groaned to a wind off the estuary. The gas radiators hissed and a glow escaped to give the faintest light in the room. The wooden chair inclined upon its back legs jammed itself under the handle of the door conveniently. Dozens of small sounds, creaks and clicks and cracks and booms combined to stir the air in the empty corridors and up the fine central staircase. On the floor above, the top floor under the slope of the roof were the empty rooms where the skivvies and maids once lived. Not a sound up there. No footfall on the uncarpeted passage that ran the width of the building. A friendly lavatory up there with a wooden seat. Where Jack sat in the dark until he was calm.

I lay and thought of Jonathan. It would all come back to him. It had to. If he told me to leave it alone, with enough conviction, then I would leave it.

I was surprised when I met him for the first time in Berlin. He was short, really short, about five foot four. I had expected a big man. A hero. Jonathan moved like an energetic chimpanzee. He had tight crinkled hair, a big nose, thick glasses, enormous teeth when he smiled, an unpleasant metallic voice and no truck with emotion or the interior life. He could have been a stand-up comic, a bookie or the chairman of a merchant bank. What you would never dream from appearance and attitude was that before you stood a fanatic in city clothing.

He was due in Berlin the day Renata left. He was coming with Beatrice. So they drifted into discussing him.

"He shouts at home."

"That is because he suffers from a crick in his neck from looking *up* at people all the time, Renata!"

"Poor Stella."

"She loves her servitude."

"She suffers."

"She is merely melancholy—by nature. She was born melancholy. I suspect that Jonathan saw something of a cause in her when he married her. She was always very kind to me but she broods. She is a fine looking woman though don't you think? Nefertiti, or do I mean the wife of Nefertiti? In any case magnificently ancient Egyptian in cast of face and sombrely Dostoyevskian in cast of mind."

"He is one who will succour the whole world and ignore the needs of his family."

"Oh nonsense. Look at me!"

"Ah, my dear boy, but you are *not* his family."

A cruel cut and Frank resists the impulse to riposte. She is going tomorrow.

"Leaving Stella," he said, "in a warm room and going out into rain and ten tenths cloud always made one feel better; not her fault."

"As you well know, Frank—she hates his mistress and has to accept the situation."

"Now that is debatable."

"No it is not. The woman is disgusting, vulgar, loud, large—and South African. When together they are a positively *bizarre* couple. He collects ex-patriates that is his weakness. He is an absurd idealist you cannot deny."

"But I do! He is extraordinarily shrewd. He has a sceptical balance of tolerance and wisdom and —— "

"And no sense. The man has no common sense. Some of the people he protects. You *know* them. Dangerous people but to him—simply refugees."

"Like we were. Like we were."

"Don't shout."

"Why not! You are having your revenge before you go!"

"They are not like us—we were *victims*."

"You try *house arrest*."

If they were English they would leave it alone. If they were English they would not have the faintest idea of what it was about in the first place. They paused to re-group.

"You are a fool, Frank. It is not your fault. You were brought up by him. The English middle class *of Jonathan's sort* can no longer distinguish between a criminal and a victim. They have failed to attend the excellent Popper. They do not understand the *necessary limits* and they have no intellectual tradition or inclination to form, and fall back on, shall we call it the ten commandments of preserving the open society. You should know better. But like them you will never know how glorious it is to be personally free until it is taken from you. Or should I say until Jonathan and his friends have given it away in the name of liberty!"

Frank was noble. He smiled, offered her a cigarette and said in an olive-branch voice, "Dear loving Aunt, do you think I forget my childhood? I believe you are simply supporting the women's cause—you punish poor little Jonathan on behalf of Stella and you make a fearful caricature of his other lady."

"Other lady! Other lady! This other lady is —— " and she spoke a sentence in German which made him turn from her in anger.

When he recovered he said, "You are too absolute. Too censorious. *Too afraid.* Don't you understand that in the face of the madness and violence of half the world . . . you will never have the knack of English tolerance. Jonathan is a good man, a really good man. Also human. So he has another lady? Also human you see. It is not a crime."

"No," she said, "not a crime. And human, I know I know. And yes I am afraid."

What she could not bring herself to say was her jealousy. He should have been her son.

Later Frank said, "I can never thank him for having me, as we used to say after children's parties. But I live hopefully. When I try it in an off-hand sort of way and say 'It was good of you, Jonathan, to include me in the family' he replies, 'Yes wasn't it!' However I'm sure that one fine day, tomorrow possibly, he'll take me to one side and say, 'Frank, not only am I about to become destitute but I'm being blackmailed and I have terminal cancer.' At last! I shall immediately track down and kill the blackmailer, find, and bring to England, a miracle surgeon from Tibet, the sort that do open body surgery with only the hands; while

Jonathan is recovering I shall invest his last hundred quid on the Stock Exchange about half an hour before the *Financial Times* Index jumps 500 points.

"In the fade-out we set off on a world cruise together. He will say as we lean over the rail (I always wanted to lean over the rail like Scott Fitzgerald), he'll say, 'I suppose you'll settle to your book, now?' and I'll say, 'Why not?' and he'll say, 'Remind me of the title would you?' which is the way the English always put it when they didn't know in the first place, and I'll say, '*Juda Verrecka*', and he'll laugh and say, 'Well! there's one that didn't' and the invisible hundred-piece orchestra will play us off the screen. Do you like that? I have a number of versions."

Renata said, "When Jonathan wants something he will ask, never fear. Then we shall see."

I slept in the great bed and dreamed. I thought there were footfalls, soft, overhead and woke. I lay confused by memories in the wrong order. Then I dozed. Frank and Jonathan leaned over the rail of the ferry as it left the pier. I swam in the water beside it. I could not keep up. Dolphins swam near me, one half grown, round and round me and somewhere to the right under the cliffs was a smashed motor car. I knew it was there. The fife band and the drummers played and the jeering Prod faces went marching by; and the black Provo berets and the dark Provo glasses supported the coffin and Frank sat up in it and waved and Beatrice shot him four times while he opened his arms to her. I could not stop it because they had me in a Romper Room. Someone said, "They even eat the dead". I pretended I was not a soldier but I knew whether I was or not they would do it. Innocent or guilty didn't come into it. I knew that. They were beyond that. That was what made me despair. All the old ideas of justice were gone and I was the last. What else can you do but wake, wash, shave, dress, go down into the silent hotel and then because nothing and no one stirs, out into the place itself to find the very image of your dream?

A ghost of a town half derelict upon a promontory. It had some life about it once, this place. For 300 years. . . .

In the car, in broad daylight above the shingle beach. Jack and Gwen.

The sea slops over on to the pebbles at the tide's edge. The sky over the estuary is banked up with clouds the colour of a boxer's eye when someone has closed it for him.

The old man in the dun raincoat leans into the car, faintly from his coat comes the smell of frying.

"Good-day sir and madam."

"Good-day."

"It is chill but fresh."

"It is."

"And it is twenty pence the ticket, lets you stay all day at this time of year."

"If we feel strong enough."

"You will keep your ticket, sir?"

"I will. Thank you."

"I hope you enjoy your holiday, you're the only one except that gentleman down there; I shall have to go down to him, that is his car isn't it?"

"I think it must be. There is nothing else from horizon to horizon except those ships out there."

"I shall lay down my bicycle and go down to him."

"Yes."

"I see from the lady's ring you are married. I was married once but my wife died. She died 27 years ago last month."

"Oh I am sorry."

"Thank you, madam, I never married again because I might not have got such a good woman. I might have got a woman that nagged me and was after my money."

"That would not do."

"It would not, madam."

"If you want to catch that chap down there —— "

"I am 80."

". . . Perhaps you'd better —— "

"I take care of myself. I never had a car, I walk and ride my bicycle."

"Well good luck."

"I expect you want this window closed against the wind."

"Yes."

"It's a lazy wind here—it doesn't go round you it goes straight through hey hey hey hey hey."

I close the window.

"I see from your ring you are married, madam."

"Yes. And since yesterday, in the afternoon, I have a lover."

"What a lucky man."

The long dun raincoat trudges bent and flapping to the shingle bank piled by the autumn storms. He labours over it. His trousers whip round his shanks. The outline of his skeletal frame dips over the other side and halts seeming waist deep. After a moment the head and shoulders of the other man rise into view. They move up a little and stand against the sky. The old man is tall, the other short. The tall figure bends politely over the other.

Gwen laughs and says, "Look, look it's Punch and Judy."

Two heads nodding. The shorter one has a big nose spectacles, is bareheaded and does not seem to feel the cold. He gropes about impatiently for his change while the old one talks and bobs. His binocular case, amber leather, gets in his way. It bumps his waist even though he has shortened the strap. The conversation is not going well for the ticket collector. Jonathan is the last person to tolerate the story of a wife dead these 27 years. None of that, old chap.

I am too far to hear or to attempt to lip read but as his head moves decisively I say aloud in a sharp dismissive tone, "Hard luck," and then after a moment, "Cheer up, you'll soon be dead."

"What!"

"Just lip reading."

"I don't believe you."

"And that shows you're no fool!"

"Do you know him."

"Not intimately."

"Who is he?"

"Frank's father."

"Oh!"

"Back in a minute."

The old man is put out. He passes me on the way to his bicycle muttering. His nose is dripping with the cold. Jonathan has disappeared under the brow of the shingle bank. I march up and over, crunching and sliding as I reach the top I get the full force of the wind. The cold gets to me and I run down the beach to where he stands near a breakwater adjusting his binoculars. He does not hear me until the last moment but I am no surprise to him. He had been watching the ferry on its way in.

"Good afternoon, Jack."

"Good afternoon, sir."

"I think you're going to be prosecuted."

"Oh yes?"

"What do you want?"

"What do you want, you didn't come for a day trip?"

"True. I came to see you."

"Out here?"

"No. I enjoy fresh air. At the hotel. I have booked there for tonight."

"Oh yes."

I give him the cutting.

"Did you send me this?"

It is no surprise to him either. He hands it back.

"No."

"Someone did."

"And a letter they tell me."

"No."

"No?"

He seems very slightly surprised.

"I lied about that."

"Why?"

"Because your daughter and your associate are both political."

"What does that mean?"

"It means daytrips to Belfast."

"Ah!" he says, "not, then, a dental technician from Dayton, Ohio."

"No."

"Then what?"

"I want to hear about Frank. I want to hear it from you. There are no circumstances in which I would betray him, dead or alive. It was suggested that I shut up because there is something to hide to Frank's discredit. If there is—tell me. But if not I shall go on with it. He did not take drugs."

"No he did not."

"Thank you."

"There is nothing you can do, Jack. The remains were cremated, the house is demolished and no one cares."

"I see."

"It will help no one to continue. Have you spoken to the press here or the police?"

"No, I was waiting for you, sir."

"Good. Then we can call it a day."

He smiles, showing his big teeth. There must be something else? Of course there is!

"We can't, sir. We can't ignore the Germans who were with him here."

I have him. I know I have him. If I can only carry it one more step.

"What Germans?"

"I have a witness, and I have photographs of one of them."

"Oh?"

"In the same way that there are photographs of your daughter and that handsome friend of hers taken in Belfast. I took those myself."

"Did you? Did you indeed! You are in that section are you? Do you torture as well? You are like the Special Branch people who come snooping around my office when I defend what they call a terrorist—whining about so-called atrocities; showing disgusting photographs; faked most of them."

"Not mine sir."

"No."

"I see."

He controls himself. It is all there in the face as it turns and juts aggressively into the wind the way the coasters out there are butt-butting into the filthy waters of the estuary.

"Photographs of the Germans?" he says.

"One of them."

"Male or female?"

"Male," I say instantly without the hesitation that would have done for me, "looks like D. H. Lawrence on a good day, if he ever had one."

He smiles.

"Yes," he says, "yes I see."

148

I cannot tell I'm there until he says, "I would like to hear your views on the Irish business".

I'll bet! I mean everyone from the Prime Minister to the Band of Hope have had their say about the Irish business, and it's only been going on for about three and a half centuries. So he must be panting to get my opinion. I do not reply.

"No one talks to the soldiers do they?"

"They prefer to talk to the enemy."

"What does that mean?"

"Long interviews with Provo leaders and para-military Prods, you must have noticed . . . sir."

"No. Have you killed anybody?"

"Three for sure."

That gives him pause.

"Did it disturb you?"

"Of course it did. Particularly the first time."

"And you believe in what you are doing?"

I let it hang. I want to take him apart. I want to ask him if he thinks he has a monopoly in causes and beliefs. I want to punish him for Beatrice and Frank's death and Peter. But he is Jonathan and but for Jonathan there would have been no Frank and without Frank where would Jack have been? It goes round and round. Also I am afraid of him. And instinct, that frail messenger from somewhere or other in the back of the head says, "Be friendly, be friendly if it kills you".

I obey. Stilted and pompous it comes out while I look him in the eye.

"I believe in what I'm doing, sir, but I wish neither you nor anyone connected with Frank any harm. I regret hitting that man and distressing Beatrice. I regret having to lie, but Frank was my friend. It seemed to me they were too casual, sir, and up to something. I felt very bad when Frank went down. I've had two months to think about it. Like you I believe in justice."

"I will speak to you this evening at the hotel."

"Thank you, sir."

"Good day to you, Jack."

Partisan he may be for liberty and equality but he loves to be called "sir".

Along the beach he goes that little strutting man towards his distant car. He is over 70 and looks 50. By God, he moves. The lie about the photographs did it. Which means that——but leave it until tonight.

My heart is pounding and I am afraid of the consequences. He is powerful. He has a daughter to protect. Adored Beatrice. There is no flaw in her in his eyes; but it is his sorrow that she has not married and given him grandchildren. And here is this ignorant soldier, this reactionary, pointing the finger not only at her but at the hoped-for husband. The loved son of the dead mistress. How it goes round. Should have been his son, but he had Frank instead before he ever met her. Poor old Stella. But perhaps she in turn has a lover. Some jolly fat fellow who never voted in his life; someone who loves her cooking. I hope so.

Perhaps he will have the police at the hotel when I get back. He's crafty enough. Press the assault charge. Harass me. Get the red caps. No he won't. He believes the photographs and their possible connections with his loved ones. Why am I sure? Because he is an arrogant little bastard but *not once* did he chop me off. Not once attempt to dismiss me after I spoke of them.

The knees are shaky after the event. Our breath steams an illusion of privacy upon the windows of the car. It is comparatively warm. I sit in silence. I become aware of her. Since yesterday I am more vulnerable because of her. I think perhaps I should drive away *now*—to reality. I turn and seize her. I put my hand between her legs. She responds at once. She is naked under the skirt, she took the things off when I was out of the car. We scramble over the seats into the back rather than let in the east wind. She is lithe and quick. She spreads for me. We do not use delicate words. We speak as soldier and whore. Skirt right up, trousers to the knees, in to the hilt, until it hurts, until the two bones grind, hair against hair, red in the face, gasping, pumping as if it is the end of the world. Covered in each other's juices, coming apart, drained, unable to move, unable to speak—then wiping each other gently gently. Joking. Hearing the sea rasp down the shingle as it gathers itself for the next advance.

It is evening and the hotel bar is doing unusual business. I have a drink in there and look them over—the passengers recently landed and the passengers who will sail towards midnight. There is nothing remarkable. No sign of Jonathan.

Opposite the bar is the window to the hotel office and the registration book lies there, open. I look at it and note his room number. There is music in the bar and it is warm at this level. From the back comes the sound of plates and knives and forks. A strange place this. As old as the town but so well built, so well proportioned that in its decline it is not seedy. It is mellow. Everything is toned down; it is full of shadows but not gloomy. As I go up the old staircase leaving the bar sounds the sense of sanctuary grows in me. The sense that this condemned old town and inn are no longer part of the rest of the country. Therefore there are no demands, no pressures—it is like a separate island and no one asks your business. It is mysterious, I felt it yesterday. It is the end of something. The couple who run the place are here for that reason. I know it but cannot explain it. It is also a place where people could starve; where violence could go unchecked among the ruins. It refuses to feel like that. It is a staging post between an island and a continent. No one but the old inhabitants and the couple have any interest in it. A most suitable place to go to ground. A most intriguing place to come upon your heart's desire. An illusion.

My room is on the second floor to the left of the head of the stairs. I have the large key and brass tag sagging in my pocket. I took it out with me. From the floor below there is a glow but my level is shadowy. Except for the faint light under my door. Perhaps someone else put the light on for me. Perhaps Jonathan let himself in because the big keys look interchangeable.

Only in films do you creep to the door, enter at the rush etcetera. I stand still and listen. I know that if I move along the passage my feet will sound through the thin carpet on the boards that were seasoned before Nelson got it from a high angle. The gun is in the glove compartment of the car. And you do not flourish guns this side of the Irish Sea unless you are desperate or stupid: but there is just the off-chance, the one in a thousand, that behind that door, waits someone who is! Or a neat package of marzipan (gelignite) with an arrangement between the hotel wiring and the opening of my bedroom door so that as I enter humming "Rule Britannia" it will ventilate me and distribute me over the walls.

151

I do not wish that to happen. I remind myself to be on my toes and I wish I had at least one of the lads with me. I sit down on the top stair and take off my shoes. Into them I put, very carefully, my car keys and change and pen and all objects that will clink. I wrap them in my handkerchief a fold at a time. I lay the heavy key on the floor.

The place where a floor creaks least is hard up against a wall. I move across the width of the passage in two. I move along the wall with my back to it, sideways a small pace at a time and balanced. I reach the frame of my door. The hinge side. I relax to stop the pounding so that I can listen. Inside my room some-one switches on the small transistor and twiddles. I do not take five minutes to work out that if he is twiddling he can't be looking and where he is there is no bomb and I'm through the door like a madman and on him and I have him flat on the floor face down with an arm behind his back and I'm saying in a high voice because I'm topped up with equal parts of adrenalin and primitive terror.

"Keep still or I'll break your bloody neck."

He makes protesting miserable sounds and I nearly faint. Literally faint. I have a feeling of stark terror and my head be-comes light and I fall sideways off him, lean against the bed and gasp "Jesus Christ oh Jesus Christ".

Frank sits up slowly to face me. The door is still wide open and it is about three seconds since I was on the other side of it.

He has a beard. Black sprinkled with grey like his hair. He wears glasses that are slightly tinted. His suit is foreign, unremark-able. He looks ten years older. Mid-sixties he looks with the beard and the glasses. I cannot say anything. I get up and go out and collect my shoes and the key and come back and shut the door. He is still sitting on the carpet.

"Well," he says, "I always knew you were devil when roused, Jacko—do your feet hurt or is this some mystic discipline from the East."

I sit down and put my shoes on. I am torn between the desire to embrace him and the urge to knock him about for making a complete and utter fool of me.

"Don't be cross," he says, "here have a drink."

I take the bottle from him. It is schnapps and it nearly pops my eyeballs on to my cheeks.

"I thought I was going to be able to give you the brief, succinct description," he says, "but somehow—I can't at the moment."

There is nothing to say. I can think of nothing to say. I sit and gaze at him. I would like to report that I am a match for the moment. I am not. Finally I say, "Where is Jonathan?"

"My goodness you did worry him."

"I meant to."

"He telephoned me last night."

"Where?"

"Holland."

"Holland?" I say.

"Yes, I live there now."

"Bully for you, chum."

"I wanted you to come and see me."

"What?"

"Well," he says, "I couldn't chance writing too soon but I rather wanted to talk to you so I sent that cutting."

"You did!"

"Yes—I thought you'd take the hint and just pop round and see Jonathan."

"Are you raving mad—pop round from Belfast to see Jonathan! A man I met once in my life, years ago. Do you know what it did to me that cutting? You—you—do you know I could be in gaol? Do you know I assaulted that bloody man Peter and outraged Beatrice and that I was going to stir it all up with the police and the press and my MP and Christ knows what else? No wonder she wasn't in mourning! Do you know that all that stuff about your mother, and three years ago in Charlotte Street you saying you might be killed in your generation *got to me*! You daft bastard. I was going to —— Listen, don't open your mouth just listen— I've been in a place where the law doesn't work; where people kill each other every day and don't get caught; where people torture each other and to add to the hallucinatory quality there are British-type buses in the streets and British-type shops and British-type money and they even speak a form of British-type speech! After a while *that* is what seems normal. You expect the smiling friendly mum—*just like your own smiling friendly mum*

153

from childhood to help her son to put a bomb up your arse. Have you got that! And there I am with my mates impartially shooting at both sides and congratulating myself that *at last* I know what you and your lot went through—*at last* some idea of the terror when the rule of law goes out the window—and I get this cutting! My old mate Frank has died a disgusting death and it is extremely fishy. So full of righteous anger and paranoia I get up on my charger and —— we'd better go out I think. We'd better go for a walk through the ruins because if we don't I'm liable to give you a hiding."

We go down and out the back way. It would make no difference if we went by the main entrance. No one will stop us. No one notices. The place is very soothing at night. The wind has dropped but it is bitterly cold and still overcast. Cats grey as fog blur away from us. Sometimes we stumble. There is a light behind the curtains at the back of Gwen's shop.

Inevitably we arrive at the bulldozed site of the house. I cannot see his face.

"They burned my books," he says.

"The surface of things are not important; not in this case. The crude events. They pass like yesterday's news. What matters is what they leave."

Our footsteps crackle over broken glass; heavy shadows full of the smell of a town rotting down to fertilize a future tourist trade (here stood a music hall, ladies and gentlemen, and here is one wall of a chapel where Wesley preached in 1794, and here the shape of a bastion—we have preserved the fire step, for infantry; in those days . . .) engulf us as if we have stepped into a cave.

"Let us tell you the crude events and get it over. I had not seen Beatrice for months. Our passion burned out for lack of trust—and Peter took her because she was at that far limit of neurosis which demands *certainty* above all. So he gave it to her. Political action, commitment. I think you knew that. She might as easily have turned to religion. It is commonplace, anyway. Of course he slept with her and he is younger and . . . that is of no importance.

"She telephoned me. Out of the blue. I could not understand why. We had parted bitterly, you see. Fortunately I was able to hear not what she was saying but something else under it. She was asking for help. After all, I've had enough practice in reading her signals. I went to see her. She was frenzied. She talked for six hours without stopping. I do mean that. About her life, her feelings—as if I did not know! Then in the early evening (I had gone for lunch) she said 'Jonathan 'phoned and asked me if I could find a bed for a member of the German anarchist Black Cross movement—on the run over here, a lot of her friends are on trial or about to go on trial in the Federal Republic. I was staggered because he sounded so casual—nothing to worry about—the lady was perfectly civilized despite the forged passport and he'd be grateful.' She was terrified by the idea. Theory is one thing . . .

"I went to see him. To volunteer in her stead. I hated the idea but I felt that *at last* there was something I could do for him. Too late. The lady—who was wanted for bank robbery, wounding a policeman and attempted kidnapping—was snugged down somewhere as an *au pair* in another part of Jonathan's net. Beatrice was off the hook.

"Next time—he rang me. 'Would I?' Yes I would. Meet them off the ferry here, perhaps rent a caravan on one of the sites further up the coast? Just a week or two. It was no problem to rent the house, you can imagine. There was a woman courier who came over with them. One of them had been brought up over here. He spoke English with a Geordie accent and a lisp! He was a big, simple lad with kind eyes. The other was dark—the one you told Jonathan that looked a bit like D. H. Lawrence. He was a lawyer, one of the common lawyers do you know about them? They're in the movement, they both participate and, when not being charged themselves, defend the others—if the judge will allow them in court.

"And the reason for this surge of German anarchists to our shores? Dear old Peter!—he makes trips over there. His net interacts with their net. Middle-class to a man, incidentally. My pair both came from rich families.

"I could not bring myself to believe that Jonathan had crossed the line. But he had. Do you know the argument? It goes like this. In capitalist countries before the war, particularly Germany, the Communists and Social Democrats handed over the keys of the kingdom to the Fascists because there was no *peacetime* underground movement and no training in resistance by force. So—anticipating the next slide to the right they, the Black Cross and others, establish underground cells to resist *now*. They show the workers (who, they say, are brainwashed into thinking that the existing order is unassailable) that the bomb, the gun, the kidnap, the assassination (and the bank robbery to finance these activities) are effective and *justifiable*. They go in for subtle arguments about what is legal and what is *legitimate* and so on.

"So, show the State to be vulnerable. Operate in separate cells. Show no mercy. The big, simple lad used to sit opposite to me and explain how much they learned last time round and how much better they will be next time. Obviously if I was putting them up and feeding them I must be on their side. So they told me they had come to execute (their word) the managing director and a number of his colleagues of the German-owned factory just up the road from here. There was a board meeting due that week.

"They intended to knock off the German directors as a reprisal for the death of two of their comrades. But not immediately. This time they intended to observe every move from the arrival to the departure of various board members and, of course, the managing director who lives in the new town.

"They both took drugs. They smoked Chinese heroin. You can't fix with it because it's impure. You remember I went into all this years ago. With the Chinese stuff, it's a reddy-brown powder, you can't judge the strength, you see. So if you fix you may kill yourself.

"The house was awful to live in. Oil stoves, cold water, calor gas cooker, camp beds, odds and sticks of furniture and this biting, damp cold coming in through every crack in the wall and the floor boards. At night they smoked the stuff and floated in their world without worry, without fear, without scruple. I liked them both. That was the worst part. The dark one used to spend hours splitting legal hairs over degrees of violence and the big, dim one used to talk slowly looking sleepily into some Utopian future for which, it seemed, he was prepared to die. How they hated, and how I would have hated, German middle-class life. The material values! But you know about that, Jack—you were there.

"They were so reasonable, so good tempered, so ready to discuss, to debate. I had to keep on reminding myself that *they killed people*. And that I was about to be, in fact already was, a party to their next attempt in that direction. I knew that if I told Jonathan (even if he knew if you see what I mean) then I would implicate him so I kept quiet. I spoke to him only once on the subject, and he said, 'If chaps like them had been around in 1933 your mother would be alive today, Frank, and we might have missed World War Two'. I did not attempt to argue.

"Then we ran out of paraffin oil. You can perhaps imagine the shambles we lived in. I went to the corner shop but they don't have it. I took the car and drove to a garage, then another garage, got a gallon of it and came back. It was dark. I went up the stairs and they had lit a fire in the grate with my books. They were smoking, sitting on sleeping bags, burning an old wooden chair they had broken up—my books were ripped apart and mostly burned. They were cheerful and dreamy. They made a space for me to sit between them and get warm. I said, 'You've burned my books' and in my head was my mother's voice about the burning of the books and in my mind's eye the newsreels of that fire that great symbolic fire and the works of Jewish authors burning to ash and I said again, 'You have burned my books'. They could have got newspapers. I had with me only about a dozen books but among them ... They said, 'Never mind, warm yourself, get more books tomorrow,' and tried to take me by the arm and I pulled away and they both got up, literally to comfort me, to calm me. They were strong, particularly the simple one and I struggled and went berserk. I was carrying the paraffin in a plastic container. It went across the room somehow and the cap was not on properly. The flames whooshed up. They did not react. The fire was immediately *everywhere*. And I ran. *And I slammed the door behind me.*"

We have stopped walking. He turns and fumbles with his flies and urgently pisses against a wall. When he speaks again I can hear that he is weeping.

"I cannot deny it to you. The others do not know but I cannot deny it to you. I meant to kill them. *Just that one action.* Slamming the door. It used to jam. Do you know what I did? I went to London by train leaving the car. I went to find Renata. She was the one person in the world that I felt I could trust at that time because you were not reachable. And when I found her —— "

"I know," I say, "I know, I saw her the day before yesterday."

"She sat before me in that wheelchair and tried and *tried* to reach out."

"Yes. She tried to tell me, too."

"Well, that's it. Jonathan took charge. I told him everything except the door. I knew that I must start again if I could. A new life. So I died! It did some good. They are not going to send anyone else to kill the Germans up the road. Peter passed the word."

"And you live in Holland?"

"I live in Holland. It's a good country. I have a new name."

"Yes I suppose so."

"I miss my chums."

"Yes."

"I rather hoped you might make the trip when you have a minute."

"Yes I will."

We begin to walk back.

"It came to me, Jack, that I do not really understand the circumstances of my mother's death."

"No."

"And that I do not really love Jonathan as he is."

"No."

"And that now I am as guilty as everybody else. Just think—I never knew I was innocent until it was too late!"

We go up to Jonathan's room on the first floor. Outside Frank says, "He'd be grateful for those photographs, I promised I'd ask."

"There weren't any."

"Oh."

"Sorry. It was in a good cause."

"Yes. It's been good to see you."

"And you. I'm sorry it was rough. You paid your debt all right."

"Yes."

Something comes to the front of my mind and I say, thinking only of myself and Gwen, "Why did you part bitterly? You and Beatrice."

He opens his mouth and when he speaks he stammers.

"All the time," he says, "I thought it was that quack, you

remember I told you, Medlock? I thought it was him playing on her instability, that hysteria, guilt you name it, to do with the incest thing."

"Yes?"

"It wasn't! That was in *me*. My feeling of somehow betraying Jonathan with his daughter. No no. Not her. She went to Medlock *second*. She met him through his partner. The Indian doctor."

"Oh Jesus!"

"Yes. I never knew. It was towards the end of the first year, that idyllic year! She never told me until about a week before I saw you that day in London. I went through all that—and she had aborted my child. No wonder she felt guilty—I mean you never quite get over something like that, do you? I'm in the same boat since I slammed that door."

"We're all in that boat. Give us your address in Holland, kid, and I'll come visiting."

He scribbles it in a little grubby notebook and tears it out; as he gives it to me he smiles and says, "I still do a bit for Eureka Records—Boris was over recently, he's got dreadfully *fat*."

From my window in the hotel I look down on the ferry alongside the jetty. The big, yellow lights make it seem like a film set because all around is derelict. My room is in darkness so that I shall not be seen. I watch Frank and Jonathan go up the gang-plank, then disappear, then re-appear on deck. Few others do that it is so cold. Obviously Jonathan is going to stay with him for a few days. There was no trouble at the little customs shed.

I stand there until they begin to cast off the lines, and she starts to slide stern first into the outer darkness.

Jonathan and Frank lean on the rail and I say aloud to myself, "Remind me of the title of your book, Frank."

"*Juda Verrecka*, Jack."

"Well, you both did and did not—that's a record!"

A tap on the door. I do not put on the light. I let her in. She comes over to the window to watch the swirl of water, see the officials get into their cars. It is beginning to snow.

"What happened?"

"I'll tell you tomorrow."

"Do you go tomorrow?"

"No the day after."

"Will you take me to London?"

"What about the shop?"

"I'll make them stock up tomorrow when they come shopping."

"Ah yes."

"I want to be with you as long as I can."

"I want that too."

She sits on the bed. With her head averted she says, "Yesterday, before I came, I went into the back room behind the shop. It's always very quiet in there except for the clock. I stood with my face leaning against the wall. I knew I would come to you and we would make love. And I knew how much I would love you and how much I would suffer for it. I said aloud—why must I go through this? Then I thought, I have no choice. Does he have any choice?"

I sit by her. I take her hand.

"I think of it quite another way. I have chosen."

The snow is falling now as it did in Berlin.